MW01119056

Imani

Ashley Robinson

To: my boo
Kiara.

From: Ashley.

Thanks for the support.

Imani

Copyright © 2016 by Ashley Robinson

All rights reserved. No part of this book may be reproduced or transmitted in any form or by any means without written permission of the author.

Acknowledgments

I would first like to thank God. God gave me the talent, passion, and the will to be a writer. Thank you God for empowering me to use the talent you blessed me with and not taking this gift away. It's been etched in my spirit since a young child. Dear father God please allows my dreams and prayer to reach your throne as I embark on this endeavor.

To my mother, what would life be without you at this very moment? If it weren't for you being a big advocate of education, I would've never found my love for words and literary skills. Thanks for loving me through my faults, my triumphs and all the moments in between. Thanks mom for being a powerful force in my life. I would love to say more about you, but the tears are swelling up behind my eyes just thinking about how awesome you are. I rather leave the crying to you.

To my father Cedric, thank you for never discouraging my dreams. You said you always knew I was destined for something above mediocrity. I must say you were right. You allowed me to explore many dimensions of myself, and I appreciate it. My father, my friend, the dreamer thanks for making me not afraid to dream and to live beyond logic and fears.

To my stepfather, I love you more than I love French fries, and we all know how much I love them. I hate the term stepfather because you go above and beyond as if you created me yourself. The love you give my mother, sisters and I give us the clearest example of what love from a man is. Thanks for encouraging my writing as a teenager when I would hog the computer for hours even when you wanted to make beats.

To my grandmother Delores, I love you to pieces. God doesn't make any mistakes. It was destined from the moment your mother gave birth to you for you to marry my grandfather and be a great stepmother to my stepdad and henceforth be in my life. You are my prayer warrior, my spiritual leader, the best grandmother anyone can ask for. Thanks for your support and prayer.

To the host of aunts, uncles, cousins…it's too many to name but thanks for calling and supporting my dream. Thanks for the countless shares on Facebook and words of encouragement. Our whole family is talented, and I plan to get us all to another level of success.

To my friends especially the ones that allowed me to vent to them during this process (Ms. Eyeconick, Octavia, Tyra, Marcus, and Taqiyya) thanks for your business savviness, encouraging words and excitement on my book. Only you guys know how critical, nervous, and excited I truly was. God bless you all in all aspects of your life.

To my friend, Jovaun I can honestly say you are the best big sister I never had. You've seen my rollercoaster life in the last year. I know because of you being my strength and prayer warrior I've managed to get this far in my life and career. I love you forever and a day boo. I will be on a plane to be at your graduation.

To my seven siblings, I love you all even if I don't say it enough. To my sister Kayla, growing up I didn't like you, but now you are my best friend. Although your six years younger than I, your maturity and heart surpasses all age boundaries. Thanks for being amazing at every role you fill – daughter/sister/friend/aunt. I know how you love and support me my future husband can't top your girl. To Brianna and Danielle thanks for the laughs and getting me to relax when I was being anal. To my brothers I watched y'all become men, and I am proud. Thanks for being supportive and protective of your nephew and me.

To my son's father, don't let this shout out go to your head but I do want to acknowledge the fact that you've been in my ear for years about getting my writing out to the world. You were the first person to read my rough cut of this manuscript and always encouraged me. Also, thanks for taking Darren off my hands to let me write.

Dear Pen sisters, there is nobody else in the world I rather share this experience with than y'all. I love how supportive we are from each other and that we are coachable. The fire that spreads when y'all type gives me inspiration daily. Keep the books coming ladies. We are team #bossladypublications for life!

To my publisher and mentor Monique Pearson, please prepare for me to get on your nerves even for future books.

Thanks for being a great listener and a true professional. You always availed yourself when I had a question or seemed tensed or insecure. You have inspired me and encouraged me to be grand in this field. You have allowed me to fall in love with all aspects of this process. Thanks for taking a chance on me and believing that I would be a great asset. To our affiliates Shan thanks for all the constructive criticism for me to be great.

Last but not least ,I have to thank my darling seed, Darren. Darren, thanks for being the air that I breathe. You are the reason I sat and decided to pursue my dreams because I need to be the best example for you possible. I see that God has blessed you with many talents, and I never want you to waste them. What a cool kid I have. No matter what work comes my way you are my priority. Even after a million books sold you would still be my biggest accomplishment.

Table of Contents

Chapter 1

I'm a grown ass woman with a fucking curfew all because niggas wanna burn CVS, Imani thought to herself.

The Freddie Gray riots had Baltimore on lock. It had been plenty of civil unrest and mayhem since this young man lost his life due to suspected foul play with police after his arrest on April 12, 2015. The ongoing mess of media calling Baltimoreans a lynch mob after the protest intensified and turned violent, causing the Mayor to institute a weeklong curfew from ten in the evening to five in the morning. Several officers were injured, plenty of people were arrested, and lots of businesses were looted before the curfew took effect. The city of Baltimore cried out for change in the most chaotic form.

Imani usually slept her days away and worked all night, but it was now 10:30p.m., and she was bored with nothing to do and nowhere she could go.

After having five blunts and five shots of Hennessey, Imani decided to play around with her make-up. She had beaten her face to capacity and taken more photos of herself than she'd like to admit. Several of them, which, she added to her Facebook page.

Of course, everyone online was just as bored as Imani.

"Hey ma, you seen my socks?" a voice behind Imani called out. Imani cringed at the thought of having a trick in her home.

The tiptoeing of bare feet hitting the floor got closer, and Imani could feel lips pressed against her ear. She spun around quickly before the trick could fully embrace her.

"Mel, your socks, shoes, and wallet is already by the front door," Imani stated.

"You're in a rush for me to leave?" Mel asked. He sat there, anticipating Imani's response while putting one leg at a time in a pair of khaki pants.

"Yes," Imani stated in a matter of a fact tone.

Mel gave a playful smile and said, "YOU can't be! You're still naked for the kid."

Imani rolled her eyes and plainly stated, "I'm in my home, and I can roam as I please. Look! Don't play the lesbian wifey role with me okay, Melanie? I mean damn, for you to be wearing the strap-on you sure are clingy like a bitch taking the dick."

Melanie a.k.a. Mel was a trick who frequented the club scene throughout Imani's life. Imani watched Mel's transformation from Jet Beauty of the Week to hardcore dom. She was about five-feet-five-inches, with light brown skin complexion, B-cup sized breasts smashed down in a sports bra, bottom row of teeth full of gold, and body covered in tattoos from the neck down. Mel's high cheekbones and green eyes were the only things that strikes as feminine.

Mel kept her hands in everything, so Imani knew she could pay to play. A conversation about Mel's failing relationship and a few shots of Hennessey landed Imani with Mel's head in her pussy and money in her pocket.

"It's like that?" Mel asked, becoming offended. Mel never knew the cutthroat side to Imani. To her, Imani always seemed cool, calm, and collected in passing. Mel frequented the clubs with her brothers all of whom Imani had a crush on. Once Mel started living in her truth of being a part of the LGBT community, she was bold enough to approach Imani. She wore it as a personal badge of honor to have scooped Imani before her brothers did. In the middle of their sexcapade, Mel contemplated making Imani the replacement for her current chick. Wishful thinking.

"Fuck you, pay me," Imani retorted. Mel walked to the front door and retrieved her socks, shoes, and wallet. When she returned, she peeled off a few c-notes and tossed them on the bed.

"You really want me gone? C'mon ma, it's a curfew and I ain't trying to get booked (locked up) for no stupid curfew," Mel pleaded.

"Not my problem. Same way you found yourself here, you can find ya way back to your lil' girlfriend who is currently on Facebook talking 'bout she's missing bae," Imani said while scrolling through Facebook on her cellphone.

Imani knew the way she was dismissing Mel was gonna cause her to cling to her at home girlfriend, in hopes of making things better, because she didn't have a shot with Imani. She also knew the girlfriend would be all too happy to wave the white flag in the name of love. She shook her head, relieved she wasn't the girlfriend. *Don't waste life being down for someone and they gonna do whatever regardless. Be down for you and stay on top of your priorities,* Imani thought as what she was taught from her younger years echoed in her head.

Mel stared at Imani as if she was an insect that needed to be squashed quickly. Imani met her stare because her 9mm was always close by. Mel turned to leave, and as she was doing so, Imani blocked her and her innocent, unsuspecting girlfriend from her Facebook friend's list. Imani didn't need any of her business exposed through social media. She tried very hard to keep personal and business separate. Although Imani didn't have any friends or family, she did have plenty of associates, and she wanted to be ten steps ahead of the game in case the chickens wanted to come home to roost. Baltimore was way too small for than anyway. Imani was no idiot. She knew social media was a double-ended sword – it could be the worst/ best thing ever.

Imani's Facebook consisted of selfies and travel photos – fairly innocent. Instagram was a whole different story. *Whatever it takes to attract the money,* Imani thought and lived by.

She could hear the front door of her condo closing, and she let out a sigh of relief. "And another one bites the dust," she said cynically out loud.

Catching her tone, she realized she used to be the sweetest girl. Imani used to have hope, love, empathy – thinking love, attachments, or bonds meant something. But, in actuality, it just hurt. She'd rather not be on the receiving end of hurt feelings.

Get what you can get out of people, which is the money 'cause you'll never get someone's heart, Imani convinced herself.

She saw her photos on Facebook were getting over five hundred likes and her inbox was full of men, and women, trying to be a contender in her love life. She logged off and rolled her last blunt, while Trey Songz's "Slow Motion" played through the Beats pill. Imani then reached for the PS4 controller.

***

December 2009

Watching Imani scurry around the kitchen in an agitated demeanor pissed Bob off, yet he tried to keep calm. Imani slammed a pot on the stove and began to mumble, "It's my birthday, and you got me fucking cooking!"

"Is there something you would like to say?" Bob asked, caressing his chiseled chin, full of his salt and peppered beard. For Bob to have been twenty years her senior, he could get more tail from a young girl than any younger man could. Bob was definitely sugar daddy material.

Over the years, Bob had molded and/or manipulated Imani – depending upon who's perspective – into what he needed her to be. Imani was definitely a Diamond in the rough. At times, she was blissfully unaware of the cosmic powers that oozed from her. She fought Bob on a lot of things, mainly out of apprehension. He had to smooth talk her, take her to etiquette classes, wine and dine her, in and out of Baltimore so she would know how to conduct herself. In other words, get the ghetto out of the girl.

"Yes Bob, I do have something to say. In the beginning, I wasn't sure about you, but you were all I had to bank on. You did so much to win me over, and now it's just clean this, suck that," Imani paused for a second, feeling like the lost little girl she'd met him as. The soft sentiments quickly faded. Not wanting to seem weak, she turned her attitude back on. She continued, "I'm just saying it would be nice to get love on a bitch's birthday."

Bob felt Imani steamed with sex appeal when she was angered.

"Come here," he said with a slight smile, flagging her in his direction.

Imani walked over, and she placed her head on his chest as Bob began stroking her ebony hair.

"Bend over!" Bob demanded, and Imani assumed the position like clockwork. He pulled her panties to the side. She only wore a pajama top and underwear around the house that day. "That's my girl," he said in anticipation.

He gave specific sexual orders with each position they found themselves in — sixty-nine, doggystyle, reverse cowgirl, missionary – just to name a few. His Caucasian frame on Imani's brown skin sent shock waves through his entire body. He was enjoying himself, and he never stopped to see if she was as well. When they were finished, a big Kool-Aid smile crept upon Bob's face.

Imani sprung from the bed that they somehow managed to get to, and headed to the bathroom, that was directly adjacent from the bedroom. Bob watched her intently as she looked at her reflection in the mirror. Imani rocked back and forth, staring at herself as if the image in the mirror would change. As if she didn't like what she saw. Her head full of her own grievances, he watched her eyes harden.

Plopping on the cold, granite tile bathroom floor, Imani began lifting a broken piece. She pulled out a bag, and in it was money – her stash.

"I'll be getting my own place this week," Imani said, eyes glued to her money.

Bob couldn't help but feel it was something he did to make her want to leave. *What is it*, he thought. Just then it dawned on him.

Imani was hoping he was a means to an end, the cure to the pain. However, he was the complete opposite. At the end of the day, he was just the same as the people in Imani's life prior to meeting him. He did care about her well-being, but he couldn't provide the love that she so desperately craved. So, why lie about it?

She would probably never show love, even if she truly fully felt it. Bob, along with the streets, had created a corrupted soul.

Chapter 2

"Fuck, they messing up the money!" ranted Caesar. Dave gazed upon his brother, watching him pace the floor in frustration, to the point Dave thought the carpet would catch fire.

Dave was well aware that Caesar had the streets on lock right now, but with the riots going on and the National Guard out, there wasn't any money to be made. Caesar continued to bitch about the situation as Dave tried to drown him out with the volume of the television.

Dave didn't know everything about the business, but he did know three things: complaining wouldn't help, they weren't hurting for money, and that it wasn't his world, so Caesar shouldn't be venting to him.

Caesar, as well as their mother, made it very clear they wanted a different path for Dave. Ever since their father died, Dave had done everything expected of him. Caesar, and their mother wanted Dave to be like a damn puppet. But he was outgrowing being a yes man.

I'm grown now. I wanna let my nuts drag a little, Dave said to himself, thinking that at the tender age of nineteen, he was such an adult.

"Nigga, turn this shit off," Caesar demanded, pointing to the fifty-two-inch smart TV that was plastered on the wall in their mother's living room.

Reruns of HBO's *The Wire* was on, and a scene with the stick-up kid, Omar, played. Caesar hated the show because it was loosely based off of actual events. To add insult to injury, Caesar and Dave's father was shot and killed by a stick-up boy.

Dave sucked his teeth, "Nigga calm down."

He grabbed his phone and proceeded to get on his addiction – Facebook. Since his mother and brother clocked his every move and were skeptical of most people, he resorted to social media and video games to pass the time.

Everyone online was talking about the same thing. *They burnt CVS. They stole from Mondawmin. Hope all cops die for what they did to Freddie. When does the Floyd Mayweather fight come on? when is the curfew over?*

It was becoming rather redundant, just like Caesar's fussing. Just then, Dave spotted her. The beautiful woman's selfies flooded through his timeline.

This girl is gorgeous, Dave thought. The young lady he was gawking over was Imani. Imani, in the picture, had a shoulder-length bang wrap. The make-up she wore made her look sun kissed.

Some pictures were only from the neck up. In the others, Dave chose to investigate, he saw a PINK sweat suit hugging

10

her slim thick frame, and the Diamond earrings shone as bright as her smile.

She was the only person on his newsfeed not talking about the riots, and that was noted to Dave. She was his Facebook crush for obvious petty reasons, like beauty, but she intrigued him due to the things unsaid. Most people plaster way too much over social media for Dave's taste.

One day I'mma tell her, Dave thought and meant.

"Earth to Dave!" Caesar waved his hands furiously in Dave's face, taking him out of his solemn thoughts.

"What nigga?" Dave answered, pretending to be agitated. The truth is, he was tickled by the nuisance his brother was being tonight.

Dave and Caesar had a great bond. Caesar was more than a big brother; he had become his father figure. Stuck in the house together because of a statewide curfew would be an experience reminiscent of their childhood before the drug game, baby mamas, kids, and random pussy took all of Caesar's attention away.

No matter how busy Caesar was, or how far apart he was physically, he always managed to call Dave or send a text message checking in on his younger brother. Or, he was wiring Dave money for gas, food, or clothes. Even his tuition was paid up, thanks to Caesar.

"You're acting, man. Where's ma?" Caesar asked, beginning to search around the house. There was no sign of their mother in the bathroom, the den, master bedroom, or the kitchen. That's actually where Caesar wished she was, in the kitchen.

Dave walked alongside Caesar out of the living room, through the long hallway bearing mocha and gold paint on the walls, and to the basement door. The knob began to turn and out of the shadows of the basement appeared their mother, Rosalyn.

"Rosalyn, you ain't hear me looking for you," Caesar taunted his mother.

Rosalyn, better known as Mama Ross, stood at five-foot-six with a mocha complexion, and brick house body with a small pudgy stomach from childbearing. Her hair, trimmed neatly in a short cut, enhanced her facial features.

Mama Ross shifted the laundry basket to her left side, "Don't start before I drop kick you in the ass!"

She always smart-mouthed her two sons. It was her way of showing love. Dave took the laundry basket out of his mom's hand and wiped the sweat from her brow.

Mama Ross brushed past her sons, trying not to tear up. It had been a long time since all of them had been in the house at the same time together. She stayed on vacation or with her grandchildren, shooting range, or gym, idly passing the time due to the fact she's a widower. Her sons were both adults, and she wasn't trying to live for them anymore.

It amazed her how her two boys were opposite sides of the coin. They both possessed an element of their father. Caesar-the street hustler, Dave- the gentleman.

"Ma I thought you don't do manual labor," Dave teased suggesting to the newly washed batch of clothes in the laundry basket he held.

"You know damn well ain't no bitch spending the night here. The maids have to go until this curfew is over," Mama Ross answered.

"Well since you're in a domestic spirit...," Caesar interjected. "Don't you want to cook for your sons?" Caesar flashed his pearly white teeth.

"Domestic?" Dave raised an eyebrow "That's the biggest word I've heard you use," Dave joked.

"Exactly and trying show those buck ass teeth," Mama Ross added to Dave's insult.

Caesar disregarded his mother, he knew his teeth were far from bucked. He took pride in his appearance and spent lots of money on it, teeth included. "I don't ever hear you using big words college boy. What the fuck am I paying for? Caesar playfully said to his little brother.

"I don't know. Maybe you can now stop sucking dick for my tuition with ya gay ass," Dave said as Mama Ross spit out the water she had just gulped, laughing uncontrollably.

"Fuck you, yo," Caesar said cutting his eye at Dave. "Oh, mama you think that's funny?!" Caesar directed his attention to his mother chasing her around the kitchen, tickling her sides.

"Get off my mama, fool!" Dave said, setting the laundry basket aside and beginning to play fight with Caesar.

Caesar knocked into the sharp jagged edge of the kitchen table, causing him to fall to his knees, and bringing mother and brother with him.

"Get y'all asses off me," Mama Ross pushed them, standing to her feet, pleasurefully guilt-ridden from the fun she had acting so juvenile with her sons. "What do you want to eat Cease?"

"Crab cakes," Caesar answered quickly.

Mama Ross started to get the ingredients when she focused on Dave, who began folding the laundry. "Dave, how much longer do you have in school this semester?"

"Ma, not much longer. Roughly about a week or so left and I'm done. Oh and don't worry my grades are cool. "Dave answered politely and proudly.

Mama Ross gave him a pound as an acknowledgment of how happy she was to hear that. *Your father would've been proud*, she thought smiling to herself.

"Yeah, I seen your syllabus online. All your finals are on a Wednesday morning," Caesar spoke. He was once again playing the role of father/big brother knowing Dave's every move.

Chapter 3

Dave sat in the computer lab at Coppin State University, watching a swarm of people parade in with stress, delirium, and fatigue written across their faces. It was finals week. He was waiting for his friends to finish the last of their finals. Having time to kill, he decided to log on Facebook.

Instantly he went to his favorite page of choice. *Miss Imani*, he thought to himself. *Am I a creep?* He questioned.

Click by click, Dave went on a journey through Imani's pictures. Vividly taking in every inch of her frame, he bit down on his bottom lip. To him, Imani was sexy and elegant. He could pinpoint his sexual desires in his loins, but couldn't figure out the flutters in his heart.

He made her his woman crush Wednesday last week with a quote from Miguel's "Simple Things" song and she liked it. Dave was extremely happy about that, but now he needed more.

I ain't trying to look like no thirsty ass nigga though. Shit, Baltimore has enough of them. Nothing beats a failure but a try, so let me level up while I got her attention and it's Wednesday again, Dave thought.

Dave reposted one of her Miami pictures and quoted Maya Angelou. He was an educated youngin' in school for Communications, hoping to land a gig with ESPN. He hoped everything he learned in school like Maya Angelou paid off for him in more than one way.

Dave swallowed the lump in his throat and pressed post. *Damn she ain't even online right now. What time is it? 3:15*, he thought.

****

The iPhone factory ringtone blazed in her right ear, causing Imani to jump up so abruptly. Feeling under the pillow for her phone, she brushed her hair out of her face and cleared her throat before answering, "Hello."

"Hey, you first tonight. Don't be late," the familiar voice on the other end said plainly. Imani hung up and flopped back on the California king size bed. She just wanted more sleep.

Glancing over at the clock it read 8:50 pm, so sleep was out of the question. However, Imani still didn't leave the bed. Tracing her silhouette with her fingers, she began calculating how much more was needed for early retirement.

Imani who was only twenty-seven years old with no kids saw retirement as very doable. It just had to be doable in the manner in which she became accustomed to.

Her extravagant Owings Mills condo, which was located in the same neighborhood as most NFL Ravens players, BMW, and a closet full of designer bags and shoes were her forever.

Over my dead body will I go back to hand-me- down and thrift store clothing I grew up in, she thought.

That was the exact reason Imani didn't have kids, she'd had a fucked up childhood and didn't want to repeat the cycle. But most importantly, children were too expensive and required unselfishness. As far as Imani was concerned, she didn't have time for that.

The same applied to men. Men took up too much time, time is money, and money gets Imani what she wants. It did get lonely for her at times, though. She was reminded every time she got into deep thought, and her fingers ended up in that soft, moist spot - like now.

Her fingers managed to slip into the purple lace heart underwear to the side and rub her clit in a circular motion, while the index fingers slid in and out while she thrust her hips. She felt herself reaching her climax and began to clutch the sheets.

"Aah," Imani exhaled.

She lazily walked to the bathroom to wash her hands and proceed to run water for a quick shower. Imani looked at the bathroom wall clock for the time. 9:30 it read. It was no time to do hair.

Her once neat wrap was now a flattened mess. Strands of sweaty hair clung to the various parts of her face. Good or bad hair day, Imani captivated attention, yet with her line of work, she felt it better to be dolled up at all times. Sex sells, and she was going to serve it to every eager buying consumer.

Guess I'll grab a wig out the walk in closet, Imani said inside her head.

The L-shaped walk in closet was Imani's favorite part of her condominium. The impeccable, organized area screamed of Imani's style and grace. Her belongings that she has accumulated over the years was perfectly displayed under the crystal white lightning and silver accented wall decor.

Clothes and accessories were grouped by agenda (sexy or casual), brand, and seasons. Rain or shine, summer, winter or fall, work or play Imani could find items easily. There were plenty of draws too to prepare for future shopping experiences.

Imani beelines back to the bedroom to retrieve her cellphone. As she walks in the closet, she looks at her notifications- Instagram, Twitter, Facebook.

It was the same old thing occurring- thirsty people. However, someone shared a picture of her, so she clicks on it.

"The beauty of a woman isn't in the clothes she wears the figure she carries or the way she combs her hair. The beauty of a woman is seen in her eyes because the doorway to her heart, the place love resides."

Chapter 4

Another dawn had come, and Imani eagerly opened the car door and tossed her bags into the empty passenger seat, causing some make-up and cash to spill out of it.

Imani checks her reflection in the mirror- *still cute,* she thought. *Cute enough to go get some breakfast. I am starving. Psst! But I don't want to go alone, and my heart is set on IHOP. Too bad I don't have any friends or a man.*

At that pivotal moment, Imani secretly disappointed in herself for becoming such a loner. It was all a defense mechanism. She never wanted to relive pain and disappoint as a consequence of forming a bond with people. Yet not forming a bond with people had a consequence too and she was beginning to notice.

Just then her pouting bottom lip curled into a victorious smile. Grabbing her phone, she went straight to Facebook. It was a quote there recently that stood out to Imani and she wanted to know the person that was clever enough to approach her in such a manner.

To Imani it wasn't the typical line she's mostly approached with such as that's bae, #wcw, she'll be mine one day, she's sexy, etc. The fact that he never went to her direct messages to talk to her spoke volumes. Those strange reasons alone Imani decided to go in his direct messages (dm).

So Imani clicked on his online name - Dave the Schoolboi, and typed "What ya name is?"

***

My plan worked. The quote I had used from the infamous poet Maya Angelou had the prettiest girl I knew message me in my inbox, Dave thought excited about the events that had taken place between him and his online crush.

Computer conversations turned into a phone conversation which quickly turned into an invite to go out to eat this morning. Of course, Dave wasn't turning that down.

Dave rushed his shower due to the fact the entire time they were on the phone Imani was already in her car while it was in park.

Throwing an outfit together quickly- blue shirt, white gucci belt, light denim jeans, blue foamposites, gold chain and blue orioles snapback- grabbed the keys to the Lexus truck and headed out.

When Dave arrived out in Reisterstown Imani was sitting on the hood of her car checking out her reflection through her cell phone.

She's vain I see, thought Dave. Then he pulled up on her, "Good morning sweetheart."

Startled Imani drops the phone in her mcm bag. "Hey," she replies with a slight smile.

Hmmm mcm bag and a BMW yeah this woman definitely has her own. A woman that has her own wants a man that got his own, Dave thought expressing lessons his mother taught him. My family has money

20

but it ain't MY money. With these thoughts, insecurity swept over him before the date even started.

"Nice wheels. C'mon and park and I'll get us a table" Imani says aa she sashayed away to the IHOP's entrance. Her Levi jeans fit her curves nicely, and her boobs were pushed up high in a t-shirt that read Cupcake Mafia.

Two minutes later Dave met her inside. The hostess escorted Dave to a window booth where Imani was sitting telling an order to the waitress. As Dave sits down the waitress walks away. "She ain't even wait to see what I wanted " Dave scoffed.

"Well you were taking mad long in the lot, and I am hungry, so I ordered for you. You're not lactose intolerant are you?" Imani asked tapping her French manicured nails against the table.

Imani's outside appearance screamed brickhouse goddess, but her grammar said typical around the way girl. *The type of girl that Dave was informed to stay away from. the same type of girls his brother Caesar had multiple kids with. Five to be exact.*

"So what do you do to have a nice car like that? Especially since your Facebook says your only nineteen" Imani ready to learn about the man who sparked her curiosity.

"Family business."

"Oh what you a trust fund baby or drug money?" Imani asked as she scanned his eyes for the truth.

Yeah, she's definitely a hood chick and ain't nothing getting last her, Dave thought. The waitress brought two tea cups on a small saucer with a lemon and tag bag draped across them and placed them gently on the table and pushed one cautiously in front of Dave the other in front of Imani. Dave waited for the waitress to be more than an earshot away to finish the conversation.

"Look it shouldn't matter. My only job is college. I'm a Communications Major, and I will be a big time producer with ESPN to keep the lifestyle I have." He watched Imani's eyebrows raise. I hope that was a solid enough answer for her.

"Your family must be proud. A man with a vision that's refreshing. Whose your family anyway?" Imani inquires.

Dave fidgets a little bit in his seat. He doesn't remember when the last time he had a date let alone a real one to be in the hot seat like this. Yet every time he glanced at Imani he was under her spell. She looked better in person and smelled great too. Her perfume carried to his side of the booth. "My dad's dead. It's just my brother, mother, and I. I've been blessed with the best, but I am sheltered. And you?"

Imani sat back.in the seat and says, "I don't know what family is. The streets raised me, and I think I turned out alright." Imani was a tad bit jealous he could use the words family and blessed in the same sentence.

"True," Dave responded.

"I know it's true, or you wouldn't have sent me that quote," Imani smiles.

Damn her smile got a nigga dick hard. "I ain't gonna fake Imani I learned that in English class hoping it would catch your attention. I've been attracted to you for months."

Dave watched Imani begin to blush as the waitress brought their meals-silver dollar pancakes, French toast, scramble eggs with extra cheese, ham, bacon, and sausage.

The food came and went, and they remained in the booth still enjoying each other's conversation and company. At this point, they seemed very at ease with one another. The endless smiles and laughs showed something very promising even to Imani's surprise whom been guarded for years.

Imani felt intoxicated-love drunk. His demeanor and style of dress melted her. The feeling was mutual, too.

"I don't care if you are a couch potato, die hard gamer, chronic masturbator, you still not beating me in 2k or call of duty," Imani said clapping her hands together for emphasis.

"you got jokes," Dave let the insults pure in from Imani. He never once gave her a full throttle response like he would've Caesar he was just in awe of how cool she was.

He had learned Imani was a twenty-seven-year-old overnight security guard with no kids working towards early retirement. She frequently travels, shops often, and isn't a big a fan of social media. Imani lied about that part being careful to not leave a scent on her trail.

Imani also told Dave she doesn't have anyone to call her friend, that everyone was an associate. That was the truth.

The biggest thing that stood out to Dave was she never had a boyfriend. "That's cool I've never had a boyfriend either," Dave joked.

Imani smiled learning that Dave was dying to get out of his family's shadow and call his own shots.

"Won't you start your own foundation or something?" Keep ya name ringing and that brings revenue to you so you can call ya own shots" Imani suggested.

Dave didn't know if this was love or infatuation he was feeling but he was feeling her.

Chapter 5

Dave walked into the kitchen high off life. The butterflies in his stomach were still dancing, and all thoughts of Imani consumed him.

As routine he turned on video games and kept his phone close by just in case she called or text or if he wanted to get on fb (Facebook). He was really hoping she would call or text him. He wanted to be addicted to her more than social media or video games.

The only reason he was addicted to social media despite his annoyance with people is due to his family constant shelling and telling him to stay out of sight.

Dave was in his own little world he never heard Caesar walk in the living room with only boxers on with his glock tucked inside.

Caesar had several properties but still managed to come back to our mother's house. " nigga it's too early for that stupid ass grin. Where you been at?" Caesar grilled Dave.

Dave squawks his eyes at his cell for the time. "It's actually two in the afternoon, and I was out ."

"Don't be a Lor sneaky bitch with me," laughs Caesar and Dave joins him.

Changing the subject, Dave asks, "Why are you waking up so late, yo?"

"Ohhh," Caesar begins while sitting down next to Dave on the couch rubbing his hands through his fresh haircut. "After some business, me and the fellas went to the strip club ran a train on a few bad bitches and I came here." Caesar wasn't ashamed in his game at all. He still needed questions answered, however, "Seriously where were you?"

"With a girl, Cease."

"Somebody from Coppin?" Caesar asked.

"Naw she's not in college," Dave admitted.

"Why not?"

"'Cause she works."

"Where?" Caesar asked in a tone spouing in disbelief.

"I don't know. She does security, though," Dave explained getting irritated. His mom and brother had a problem with most people he tried to befriend. They were so jaded by the street life they didn't trust a soul. Mama Ross and Caesar would rather the snakes touched them before ever touching Dave. For that purpose, alone, Dave's college friends he only hung with at college and the ladies he just fucked.

It wasn't many females after him since he wasn't a socialite and was a heavy gamer. The cat always got the attention though and the fact most women said he favored the actor Larenz Tate. But those were the women that were only worthy of a good lay. However, Dave mainly wanted to save those females the harassment from his family if they ever intended on getting close to him.

"Security huh? She must be an older broad that means she wise enough to run game on ya stupid ass," Caesar hissed.

Dave remained quiet focused on the ps4. He was so into Imani already that he wasn't for Caesar's shit. After one date she had him.

"Let me see a picture of her?" Caesar asked, and Dave obliged by clicking on Facebook, tapped her profile, and tossing Caesar the phone. "Hold tight! She looks like the stripper from last night." Caesar exclaimed starring closely at the phone. He studied and examined her through the picture. Dave stayed silent. "It's definitely her, 'cause I don't forget faces or a body like that."

Dave's heart ached, and he cringed at the thought of his brother being right. she's a security guard she wouldn't lie to me about that. The feelings that brewed for Imani wouldn't allow Dave to belief anything different.

Caesar burst out into laughter never recognizing the disarray Dave's emotions and mental was in. "You got played youngin' she's a stripper with a bad rep by the name of Infinity or some shit yo. She got a tattoo on her ankle and a birthmark on her ass. So just fuck her and be done with it."

"Man fuck outta here!" Dave spat and stormed out leaving the ps4 on and forgetting his cellphone. He walked to his car and just sat there. Dave wasn't worried about anything except the situation at hand.

Damn I got it bad for her, he thought, realizing he cared about this information Caesar gave him.

Twenty minutes later Caesar knocked on the window so Dave cracked it. open Caesar threw Dave's cellphone through the car window and walked away without saying a word.

Dave watched as his big brother got into his vehicle and disappeared into the distance. *I gotta get to the bottom of this shit now*, Dave thought with worry striking his mind and heart. He dialed Imani's number.

"Hello?" She answers groggily.

"You're a stripper by the name of Infinity with a tat on your ankle?"

Chapter 6

Dave sat in Imani's living room skimming through magazines of hers. She peered at him from the guest bathroom, and she could tell he still wasn't at ease with her answers.

Imani was pissed that there were already trust issues between them, and they just started connecting. Any other person she would've delivered her truth, but she liked him too much to taint the image she had in his eyes. On top of that, she secretly hoped that quote he used for her rang true. Unfortunately, she didn't feel as though she was worthy or beautiful without material things.

You can always tell him the truth; you can always curve him. Fuck what he thinks, she tried to lie to herself. It's something about him however, and I know he'll be good to me. I can just feel it. But Baltimore too damn small for the drama his brother is creating. Granted Dave warn me that his family be in his bushes (business) but damn. That shit will have to end I won't fake like I don't like having control over everything in my life. That would include Dave too. His family and I can't share reign, Imani debated and plotted in her head.

Imani had let Dave know that she had a twin sister that she doesn't have a relationship with. "She strips and I don't have a tattoo on my ankle" the lie flowed freely and easily off of Imani's tongue as she showed him "her" Instagram page.

At that moment while Dave was totally engulfed in the supposite sister's Instagram account Imani excused herself to the bathroom. Imani assumed that Dave thought she was taking a shit because she had locked herself in the bathroom for thirty minutes continuously struggling with her conscious.

She did, however, get something accomplished in the bathroom. In two minutes flat, she changed her outfit. The remaining twenty-seven minutes she just stared at Dave from the crack of the door observing his mood, seeing if her lie settled as truth.

Imani finally got the nerve to step out and strut over towards him. I stood in front of him silently and allowed the silk hipster black robe fall to her ankles exposing her birthday suite.

The tension between the two made Imani shift her stance awkwardly.

Dave stood up from the couch and motioned towards Imani and planted a thick kiss on her. The kissing was nonstop, and they took shallow breathes in between. Dave picked Imani up, and she pointed to the bedroom where her California king bed awaited them.

Soon as he dropped her on the bed, she felt the stiffness of his manhood, and he was indeed blessed. As he stripped it was confirmed- he was the size of a horse.

Imani kissed his chest loving his almond skin and made her way down. He moaned from the oral that she performed. His body tensed and she knew he was about to come and when he did she allowed to slide down to the back of her throat. He stared at Imani with pure astonishment.

Imani laid back and started playing with her pussy. This performance made his manhood stand at attention again.

He thrusted inside of her and instantly found her g-spot. That's never happened before, Imani thought happily. She began to shake, and tears of joy swelled behind her eyes.

In and out, in and out he rocked, and Imani took it all. He was well endowed so at times it was painful, but she didn't complain. Pain is pleasure and pressure bust pipes. She came, he came, end of discussion.

Imani lay on his chest as Dave stroked her hair. "Do you wanna be my girl?" He asked. Imani just smiled as her way of accepting and fell asleep at peace.

Chapter 7

Dave never left Imani's side after settling a score with passionate, thrilling sex. Being on cloud nine there was no place he'd rather be.

Imani never had a person in her space for days at a time but she agreed to be his girlfriend, and she wasn't turning back. Dave was sweet, funny, and exciting. The most exciting part is the sex. They had sex all the time. Sometimes for no reason at all. For the times it was reasons, it was all a challenge- couple's coupons from Spencer's, waging on sports, betting on video games or playing family feud. It had become very fun and entertaining.

Dave loved the way she held his shaft with the left hand and stroked the head of his penis with her right all the while slurping sloppily and hungrily on his entire manhood. She would spit on it from time to time causing him to ejaculate all over Imani's face. Anything close to her lips he licked off the rest was wiped away with a warm rag Dave retrieved from the bathroom. *Mmm, that's my nasty bitch,* Dave thought, helping Imani wipe his milky white residue off.

"Hey babe get dressed," Dave said smacking Imani's round ass as she rolled over on the bed clutching the sheets preparing to take a nap.

They had sex all night the night before, and it poured over to the morning. Imani's eyelids were low, and body felt like silly putty-loopy and worn out.

Dave laughed at himself at the job well done. Imani was no slouch in the bedroom either. He loved the fact that she was his personal porn star. Anything that he has ever seen or masturbated to through online porn she did without asking. Although he wasn't a virgin, he had done the basics a time or two in the past, but Imani's zest made him feel like a virgin. For that reason, alone, he was happy to have, love, and spoil her no matter how drained himself he was due to their overnight gut wrenching, uninhibited love making.

"Imani forreal get up! " Dave said assertively causing Imani to peek at him with a lazy smile.

She was secretly getting wet all over again from his take charge tone. " what you gonna do for me if I get up?" Imani began to crawl sexily off the bed towards Dave. Like a lion on a gazelle, she was ready to pounce. Her body didn't seem so weary suddenly.

"I'll eat it in the shower before the real surprise" Dave answered with a megawatt smile brushing his hands against his own naked flesh.

And like a group of kids chasing each other on the playground Dave and Imani ran and disappeared into the shower.

While in the shower Dave's phone vibrates from a text message from Caesar. It read I tracked your car down in front of your college buddy's house near the campus by your not here. I will find you and that Bitch.

***

Caesar's blood was boiling at the lengths his younger brother was going through for a chick. A chick Caesar believed was low down and dirty. He would go to the ends of the earth to prove it.

A text message flashed across Caesar's phone screen. He had hoped it was Dave but to no Avail. It was Jodi saying 15.

Personal affairs would have to wait there was business to attend to. There was disloyalty amongst the ranks and too many supposition stick ups around a particular neighborhood.

Caesar was well aware of his troubles with the Black Guerilla Family - a gang of ruthless young black man using their power from jail and trickling into the streets of Baltimore. murder and mayhem followed them. Jodi and Caesar planned to do whatever to live another day and keep the cash flowing.

When Caesar got to his destination, he could see Jodi and a few young soldiers on a roof top holding two men hostage.

****

Dave admitted to Imani he didn't want to be found so she had to drive her car.

"We got to stop for gas first" Imani stated pulling into the first gas station she saw.

"Hope you don't think you're using those pretty manicured hands to pump," Dave said.

Imani pulled in front of a pump and put her BMW in park. "Guess your pumping then" Imani smiled. She pulled her wallet out and removed her phone from the aux cord. Imani was halfway out of the car when Dave tugged at her arm.

"Where are you going?" Dave asked confused.

"I am going to pay for the gas," Imani stated.

"Psst! Girl sit your ass down," Dave demanded getting out the car to pump and pay for the gas being the gentleman he only knows how to be. Once he was finished, he hopped back into the girl, "make this right."

When they arrived at their destination, they both smiled looking at the beautiful building. Dave had wanted to do something different to keep Imani's interest. He didn't want to look like a child to her provided the age difference, therefore, he googled this Jazz and R&B day party.

After parking, they both walked to the entrance side by side. Dave was careful Imani was on the right side of him. It's the gentleman thing to do. In case something came their way he could protect her. Unbeknownst to him Imani was doing the same ever so often stay a few steps back in stride to watch his back.

"Rose for the lady?" The host asked. Dave bought three and handed them to Imani. With each step, they took they were greeted with another host handing out champagne, hors d'oeuvres, and chocolates.

The inside consisted of high arched ceilings, wall to wall brown carpet, gold chandeliers and various ice sculptures down the massive hallway. A host walked them to stain glass door which led outside to the botanical gardens.

The botanical gardens were gorgeous, too.

Imani and Dave found some seats. Dave pulled the chair out for Imani to sit in and he couldn't help but to watch her round behind slide down in the seat. Her all white romper glued to the perfection of her curves.

"Is this alright?" Dave asked hoping she didn't think he was corny. Imani was swaying in her seat to the sounds of the Why Lie Band.

"It's nice. Glad to see you have layers. Then again what can I expect from a college kid," Imani joked placing her hand over his.

"Would you like a picture?" A photographer asked standing in front of them.

"Sure," Imani said moving in closer to Dave. Dave wrapped his arms around her for their photo op.

"Are you going home tonight?" Imani asked.

"No, I'll go back tomorrow," Dave replied grasping Imani's hands.

Chapter 8

Caesar sat on the corner of Baltimore and Hilton watching his business flow properly. He was also making time past until it was time to scoop one of his youngins off of pen Lucy to go on a mission. He wanted to once and for all prove to his naive younger brother, Dave that he was fucking with a deceitful woman.

His frustration over the situation grew because he and their mother taught him better than that. Caesar however never talked to Mama Ross about this situation. He wanted it handled man to man.

He ain't supposed to fall prey to the game whether it's drugs or women. He posed to be better than me, ma, and daddy. God rest his soul, Caesar thought.

Judging by the text Dave sent several days ago he wasn't listening. It was a picture mail with Dave and "Imani" laid up in her bed, you got the wrong girl kid, and she's all mine.

Not if I have a say so, Caesar thought angrily crushing the soda can that was in his hand. Dave never responded to Caesar's text message earlier, and he took the location off his iPhone so he can't be tracked.

"K.O. come here woe," Caesar called out to one of his young boys. K.O. comes over to Caesar immediately. As he approached, he could hear some random kid screaming, "Loud packs! Loud, loud, loud."

"Sup big homie," K.O. greeted Caesar as he leaned on Caesar's car with his back turned to him and eyes on the product.

Caesar loved that he trained his youngins to be alert at all times. Caesar always preached never let bystanders, kids, women, friends, or even himself keep ya eyes off the business or surrounding.

K.O. wanted to be a boss. In the future, it was quite possible but next in line was Jodi if Caesar was ever booked (arrested), retired, or lullabied(killed). Mama Ross and Caesar already discussed this.

"Man, I'm about to get up out of here. Jodi and I will meet y'all later for the count and reup." K.O. nodded and walked away to Caesar's words. Caesar sped off and into the iPhone he said, "call Jodi."

Jodi answered after the Third ring, "Yo!"

"I'm on pen Lucy c'mon," Caesar responded.

Jodi was like a little brother turned best friend to Caesar. They made money together and did their whoring together. Jodi was only twenty-three years old, seven years younger than Caesar but he was an old man at heart. He's seen a lot and been through a lot.

With that being said he's the only one, Caesar felt comfortable asking doing this favor- mission break up Dave and Imani.

40

Caesar briefed Jodi on the situation "yeah yo she playing my bro." Jodi was glad he told him the story because he naturally assumed they had to rid more BGF niggas for killing their member and being on their turf in east Baltimore. today was about family business only.

Jodi and Caesar are no strangers to strip clubs. They have heavily frequented Vegas, Miami, and stadium in D.C. They have been sticking closer to home lately going downtown to Norma Jeans. That's where I know for sure I've seen "Imani," thought Caesar still not believing that was even her real name.

The plan was to go to the club, blend in with the crowd, and when she was spotted have Jodi proposition her and smut her out. Caesar would lure Dave to the spot to catch Imani in the act. Therefore, he would have no choice but to face the truth.

By this time Caesar and Jodi had been in the club for two hours puffing on cigars, popping bottles, throwing Benjamin's and still no sight of her. The club ends at two it was now one-thirty in the morning. "Damn she probably not here tonight," Caesar leaned over to Jodi and said over the loud music as the strippers were caressing their frames. they were relentless to get that last dollar in.

"Hold tight Big C they might know something," Jodi replied. Jodi flashed his pearly white teeth while his bottom row was laced in rose gold Diamond grills. He addressed the strippers, "hey ladies y'all know where infinity at?"

"Why are you asking about her when you should be seeing what's up with me and you." one stripper spat. She was 5'2" with an hourglass figure dressed in a PINK sports bra and black thong and six inch heels. Colorful flower tattoos covered her left hip. Jodi just grinned harder.

The club was letting out, and everyone filled the parking lot and nearby streets. Some of the dancers now dressed in sweat suites swarmed around Caesar and Jodi. They were regulars. They knew Jodi and Caesar had good dick and fat pockets.

Since the mission was unsuccessful, Jodi and Caesar both had easy pussy on the brain.

Jodi had his back turned to Caesar stroking a girl's ego, and Caesar was doing the same with another girl. All of a sudden shots rang out, and it seemed like too many to count.

Caesar could see feet zooming past his face as he dropped to the ground. The sounds of screams and panic became faints as he heard a voice say, "BGF muthafucker."

Caesar never saw the persons face, just blood splatter stained t-shirt which means he was in close range to his victim-Caesar! *I was caught slipping, not paying attention going against my own rule*, Caesar thought as the pain took over his body.

His eyes were getting heavy, and he could see a blurry Jodi shaking violently going into shock.

Just then Caesar heard police and ambulance sirens faintly in the distance before he heard one last pop!

Chapter 9

Planning her son's funeral was a heart wrenching experience for Mama Ross. planning her husbands was enough. But with the game they were in, she knew it came with the territory.

Thank god I didn't have to plan Jodi's too, she thought.

Jodi was still in the hospital and is expected to survive even after the massive blood loss.

Dave had been holding up better than expected he only had one major meltdown, and that was in the coroner's office.

Dave kicked and screamed crying an ocean full of tears over his brother's cold, lifeless body. He pulled himself together largely in part of to Imani who has been by his side every step of the way. Imani waited on Dave and Mama Ross hand and foot.

Mama Ross wasn't naïve however. She didn't survive the streets of Baltimore and become a hustler's wife being stupid. She could sense Imani had some shit with her.

Caesar and I been warning Dave all his life with every line in the book. Hell bitches are snakes too. Women will get you caught up the fastest. Most importantly never trust a big booty and a smile.

Mama Ross always wanted a good girl for him. Someone just as sheltered and naïve as him to keep him away from the lifestyle his daddy created.

I must say Imani is playing the role of a good girl very well to the deceitful eye. I won't label her as a snake just yet, but she's definitely not innocent or naïve. She's around the way girl. However, I respect the care she has for my son. I see that in her eyes. I also see a natural born hustler too.

The repass was over, and Mama Ross house finally was clear with the exception of Dave, Imani, and two of their street soldiers.

Imani walked over with her red bottoms clicking against the granite. She handed Mama Ross a folder and then removed her Gucci sunglasses and tucked them in her blouse, "Your lawyer said all of your travel papers are inside."

"Did you look inside?"

"No mam it's not my place" Imani stated candidly.

Mama Ross smiled. This girl is good, she thought. She opened the contents of the folder and tossed them to Imani.

Imani placed her black matte manicured nails on top of the papers with a confused look. Ever been to Turks and Cacaos?" Asked Mama Ross.

***

The boat swayed from side to side, and the sun melted Mama Ross' skin. It reminded her of the time her dear departed husband took her for the first time. Back when it wasn't popular for Black's to travel.

Mama Ross remembers screaming like a school girl at every new experience she encountered at Turks and Caicos. However, that year the humidity was so high she received a

44

painful sunburn patch on her thighs for the entire trip. But that was the least of her worries because she had arrived.

She had come a long way from the nerdy orphan turned stash house provider to king pen's wife.

Her parents were alcoholics and died in a head on collision. she was about thirteen and was admitted into foster care where she stayed for only two years. Mama Ross ran away tired of constantly physically fighting every day because she was a nerd. She was quiet and withdrawn trying to cope with her parent's death. Rosalyn almost felt like they left her on purpose. The thing her parents taught her helped her pass the time she kept her head in the books.

She had hoped all the knowledge she gained from books would make her feel and turn into a somebody instead of a piece of shit.

One day after fighting this girl by the name of Evelyn, Mama Ross ran away from foster care and lived on the streets. She slept under bridges by night and in the mornings would go to McDonald's bathroom to wash up and walk to any hotel that served Continental breakfast and blended in with guests.

That was her routine for several months until a hotel clerk suspected something. " excuse me, girl, where are your parents?"

"In the room," a younger Mama Ross lied scoffing down eggs.

The hotel employee raised an eyebrow, "what room!'

"101," Rosalyn spat.

The clerk disappeared, and five minutes later she returned. " I am going to call child protective services. You are clearly lost and unsupervised. Besides room 101 isn't booked."

Mama Ross heart started to pound as beads of sweat started to form on her forehead. The fifteen-year-old Ross knew if cps (child protective services) was called she would be back in foster care or worse.

A raspy voice cleared his throat behind Mama Ross, "hey niece I've been looking for you.

Rosalyn turns around to find an older handsome gentleman about 6'5," medium built, wavy hair and he wore a business suite.

"Is there a problem?" He addressed the clerk.

"Not at all Mr. Evans," the clerk walked away quickly, and Rosalyn took note of his power.

"Thanks, mister," Rosalyn said shifting awkwardly.

"Do you need a place to stay?" Asked Mr. Evans and Rosalyn nodded yes hoping that he would be her savior. And he became just that. He had put her in a house in the projects cutting and stashing the product. Eventually, the savior became a lover and best friend, father to my children, husband to me - Joel Evans.

Mama Ross was broken out of her thoughts from the past when Imani called out, "Mama Ross your real relaxed huh?"

"Don't call me that! Call me Rosalyn."

"Well, Rosalyn thanks again for inviting me. I am glad the trip is doing everyone some good under the circumstances," Imani said adjusting her lavender two-piece bikini.

Mama Ross motioned her to sit next to her. "Look I'm not about beating around the bush. We only came here to let the heat die down. Knockers (undercover police) gonna be on high alert and so is our enemies that took my first born from me. And I don't know about you, but I'm too strictly dickly for jail. Besides, I want to see my grandkids grow up before I die."

Imani listened intently as mama Ross continued "I'm pretty sure you've guessed by now what my family does. Dave's dad was a king pen. Caesar took over. I don't want this for Dave at all! Jodi is next in line, but he's a vegetable at the moment. I as the queen doesn't need to be doing manual labor or dirt. So I am propositioning you to take over as Queen pen. I've observed you. You have your own money, so I know you won't be shiesty. You're not naïve either so I trust you won't be swindled. Plus, my son loves you and trust you which means you can keep him in school and out of this life while keeping the money flowing. Do you think you want the position?" Mama Ross asked Imani never blinking.

"Yes," Imani answered eagerly.

"You fuck up this business or break my son's heart I will end your life personally!," Mama Ross threatened.

Chapter 10

When returning to the States, Imani never said anything to Dave about the talk Mama Ross and she had. She thought maybe Mama Ross would be responsible for dropping that information in his lap. But just in case she didn't give him the news Imani had her own plans.

In the cab from BWI airport to Imani's condo, Imani flung her long plats called goddess braids and turned her attention to Dave. "Baby, how are you feeling?"

"It's gonna be a long summer," Dave huffed looking onto the barrage of traffic and familiar scenery of his hometown. Having to face the reality that he wouldn't see his brother again.

"I know what you can do to make it better," Imani said knowing that this idea would never dismiss the hurt from losing a loved one but at least it would keep Dave occupied.

"Yeah right," Dave said in disbelief. He had a fairly decent time in Caicos, but he didn't have much optimism to go off of. He was just trying grieve one day at a time.

"Baby seriously I have a plan. Won't you start a foundation? It can be similar along the lines of black lives matter. Use your testimony to uplift others. We can use social media and fliers as well as your college circuit to get the word out. We can have a big event at a hall - food, music, games, and a panel to address the issues. Most importantly it would be your business no longer will you be in your family's shadow," Imani said using his wants against him.

****

A month later the foundation was totally underway. Dave had rented out a downtown Baltimore conference room to have his first ever event in.

The word was buzzing thanks into a large part of social media and Dave's Coppin supporters.

While Dave was working the room, he noticed some of Caesar's loyal associates to trying to support Dave out of respect for the deceased Caesar. Everyone knew how much Caesar loved Dave.

Imani wasn't far behind as Dave said his hellos and thank you for coming. She wore a canary yellow Marc Jacobs business suite with a big, colorful necklace that draped her entire breasts.

"She's beautiful," random onlookers said to Dave as both Imani and Dave smiled humbly at the compliment.

Mama Ross walked over to them, "It's your turn to speak before the panel starts Dave."

"Ok ma," Dave kissed both his ladies- Mama Ross and Imani on the cheek and headed towards the front where the panel and the microphone awaited him.

The DJ halts the music, and the chatter seemed to slowly stop. Dave lifts the mic up to his moist lips, "I would first like to say thanks to everyone who came today. I never done this before but I was raised to be different to be better. With all the senseless acts of violence due to law enforcement or our own hands, it's time to teach others to be better be different.

The speech Dave gave may have been lengthy for some peoples taste, but it was pure from the heart the only way Dave knew how to be. Plenty of mothers, fathers, and sons thanked Dave and took pictures with him. They even asked for resources to channel their kid's anger or get them scholarships in which Dave gladly wrote checks to those in need. They were pulling on his heart strings.

Imani and Dave were among some of the few last to leave. They held hands walking to his car. "Mhmmm, I love a man in a suite" Imani said while her eyes lustfully looked upon Dave in his black tom ford suite. At first, he didn't want to wear a suite thinking, he would be overdressed for a summit, but he wanted to be perceived as a business man and influence the next generation to be different. He knew how his family got their money was wrong. But he didn't do it personally, and they never took a life that didn't have it coming.

Sitting in the car, Dave replied to Imani, "This suite won't be for long." He put the car in drive and leaned over for a kiss when suddenly, glass shattered, falling on both Imani and Dave.

"Pull of, pull off!" Imani screams as Dave drives frantically swerving into parked cars. In the dashboard, Imani sees a bullet lodge in. That could've been us, she thought. She scouted around to see if they were being followed. She sensed that they were.

"Make a left," Imani demanded, watching a black sedan pursue them in the rearview mirror.

"What?" Asked Dave frantically.

"Baby, do you trust me?" Imani asked realizing Dave was scared shitless.

"Huh? " Dave questioned. This isn't the time for deep talks. He just wanted to get out of dodge.

"Do you?!" Imani screamed reaching in her purse for her favorite toy- her 9mm.

"Yes," he answered still driving to no particular destination.

"Then shut the fuck up and make four lefts," Imani watched Dave weave in and out of traffic running red lights, and he finally made four lefts which caused them to go in a circle. It was exactly Imani's idea. "Now put the car in reverse and ram the sedan!"

Dave obliged going from zero to ninety in reverse smashing the front end of the sedan causing a three car pileup into an apartment building wall.

Imani and Dave both was experiencing whip lash, but Imani mustered enough strength to get out of the car.

She hated the fact that they just left a function full of positivity speaking against violence, and they were in this situation. However, she knew being positive drew haters just as well as flashing wealth did. Baltimore was full of crab in barrel type of people and Dave handing out checks probably made him a target. Imani needed for her and Dave to make it back to the condo alive.

The closer she got to the crashed up sedan she saw BGF Flags around the steering wheel. The driver was unconscious blood dripping from his temple. The passenger stiffened fidgeting for a gun that fell to the car floor, but Imani left off two quick shots.

The street they were on was a small street with not a lot of traffic and Imani trusted any witnesses wouldn't dare come forth. "Come on," Dave shouted, and Imani jogged to the car.

Dave zoomed off with his bumper barley attached. "What the fuck were you thinking? In front of an apartment building with no mask?"

"I was thinking it's either them or us. Baby, I'm not losing you like you did Caesar. If you fight I fight if you die I die," Imani said with tears feeling an unknown feeling- love.

"What do we do now?" Dave softened his tone.

"Pull over," Imani stated and when he did she walked to the nearest Storm drain. It pained her to have to do this, but it was too risky to keep. She dropped her gun and watched the sewer wash it away.

Once back in the car, she clutched Dave's hand trying to take away all of his anxiety, "we got to get rid of the car let's go to a junk yard."

Chapter 11

It had been a year since Caesar died and Dave and Imani were still going strong. Dave had a year left until graduation and then he would be off to his internship with B.E.T. Imani has all the while been keeping up with the money.

Imani had total reign over Dave just the way she wanted. She loved the fact he still treated her like a queen, and the sex was still phenomenal.

Mama Ross stayed out of the hair as long as the business was cool and their safety wasn't at risk. She found out about their run in with rival gangs months after many causalities.

Mama Ross had told them casualty was bad for business and Imani handled right away being so coachable. At that moment Dave found out Imani was taking over Caesar's position as a favor to his mother. He wasn't happy about it but the way Imani handled herself in the face of danger and some pussy thrown in his lap it wasn't nothing he could dispute. Although he was still surprised by his mother's actions. Mama Ross did reveal somethings to Imani about her childhood. They had similar stories.

Imani still did "overnight security" to keep up appearances. She could've retired months ago, but her shopping habit has become ridiculous.

What was also ridiculous she could've come clean about her double life. Imani had plenty of opportunities to come clean. However, for the first time in a long time. She didn't want to say her truth out loud. Dave wasn't a trick that she was conditioned to keep at bay. It was a spark there. She didn't want the spark to diminish because her life been bullshit after bullshit. In actuality she thought, I may be doing him a favor of keeping him away from my mess.

Futures march madness blasted through the speakers of the rental car Imani picked up for her travels. She turned the volume down when her phone started ringing. "Hello," she answered.

"How long are you gonna be gone again?" Dave whined into the receiver.

Aww, my baby misses me she thought. "Boo, I just touched down in Houston. I'mma set up shop then I'mma do the same in Atlanta and Vegas. Give me a week at least," Imani said and her line beeped. It was K.O. "hey Dave let me call you back."

"Be safe? " he says as Imani clicked over to K.O.

"Yes doll," I said to K.O. Imani and he had built a friendly rapport. He was all about the money. Didn't hurt to have him around as eye candy as well. K.O. was darker skinned, but his skin always glistened so healthy, full lips, straight and white teeth with facial always trimmed neatly. Of course, he was younger than Imani but so was Dave. For that reason, alone, it was just easier to deal with than Jodi.

Jodi has recovered, and he's still in the game, but he hates answering to Imani. But he doesn't complain cause his pockets were fat and Imani had made allies with their former enemies. He can't say pussy ain't power.

Imani's manipulation skills were on point and Caesar, and Jodi had trained the young boys well to be hitters. Any nervousness Imani felt in the beginnings taking over quickly faded.

She was definitely in the position to be a queen. The power was a drug. Imani felt herself changing on the inside becoming worse but on the surface, she kept her composure.

"Where you?," K.O. asked.

"Be there in an hour to meet" Imani hung up. She was actually en route to the strip club. K.O. was very trustworthy, but she didn't need him there yet. *Never let your left hand know what your right hand is doing*, she firmly believed, as the words rung in her head.

The black "damn Gina " crop top blew in the breeze as her hips swayed in the high waist jeans. She had a brand new nine tucked in her jeans, the other in my purse and a knife tucked in her Jordan's with a razor under her tongue. She was cautious and strapped no matter what.

Imani opened the strip club door and walked down a dim lit hallway making her, way to the owner's office.

*Knock, kno*ck. The office door opened, and Imani stepped in.

"Imani, meet the Mayor, and meet the club owner Mr. Richardson," Bob spoke. He wore a t-shirt that read, "Put some respeck on it."

Irritated Imani rolled her eyes. *Clown*, she thought and she then she turned her attention to the two gentleman- the Mayor, and the owner with a smile.

"Imani and I've known each other for years but these last six months she's been co-owner of my strip club in Baltimore. It is very lucrative. She wants to expand all of her business ventures. That is why we called this meeting today," Bob further explained.

"She's not dressed for business," the Mayor rudely stated.

"I'm dressed for my environment. This is a strip club in the hood what other way is there to look?" Imani shot back in a matter of fact tone. Bob nudged her, and she immediately flinched having a flashback of an unpleasant time.

"What do you propose?" Mr. Richardson asked.

"Look, Mr. Richardson, I want to partake in ownership of your club I can guarantee prettier, curvier girls as well as promoters and themed events. You'll be making more money than ya spend."

"How do you plan to do that? I am doing good already." Mr. Richardson was inquisitive.

"How about doing excellent? I run the heroin game in bmore we expand out here and add a brothel to your club and better strippers. The Mayor can guarantee us to not be shut down or raided everyone is getting paid with their dicks sucked if he's on board. Trust me, you and the Mayor will receive the biggest rewards." All three men chuckled as Imani finished her game plan.

The Mayor gripped Imani's ass and Bob locked the door.

***

One hour later K.O. and Jodi met Imani at the strip club in the dressing room. They walked in as Imani was passing some females their new uniform which consisted of black knee highs, black crop tee, black thong and a ski mask. Everyone that wore this would be a part of the brothel. Meaning you were down to fuck for a buck and that buck better had some zeros behind it. Best believe Imani wanted her cut too.

Call me a queen pen/pimp if you wanted just know I'm never going back to broke, she thought.

Jodi stared as the beautiful women changed right in front of them. The construction workers were there too expanding the building for a boom boom room where anything goes.

"Jodi I want you to stay here and oversee construction and make sure these bitches can be trusted with the product 'cause you know the same motherfuckers paying for pussy is the same ones down to get high So we can jam off here. I just don't need no rats or thieves among us. You are good at weeding people out," Imani said to Jodi.

"Don't I know it," Jodi replied looking at Imani in pure disgust as usual. He walked to the corner observing the construction workers.

"K.O. dear, follow me" Imani walked to the opposite corner of Jodi so that he couldn't see nor hear the conversation she wanted to have with K.O. K.O. followed her. "I want you to find somewhere here in town that can keep an eye on the product when we ain't here. That's normally Jodi's position, but I'm making it yours."

He shook his head okay and reluctantly said, "Make sure that nigga know that, 'cause he be tripping."

"I got you," Imani grabbed his shoulder, and his body tensed. She could see a print emerging in his jeans and Imani was sure it wasn't a gun. Imani always knew he found her attractive, and she did him as well. Can't lie I'm curious about him. Now that a man finally made me cum I wonder how many others could cause for years I've been backed up, Imani thought biting her bottom lip. She tried to suppress the urge, but I gotta do right by Dave and not fuck the help.

However, the freak in her was hard to die. Imani brushed up against K.O.'s hard dick and caressed the tip of it with her hand peering over her shoulder to be sure Jodi wasn't looking. "I'mma go to the hotel and play ps4 before my flight to Atl. I'll send for y'all." K.O. swallowed hard and didn't respond.

Imani was walking out when she saw Jodi fiddling with his phone, but Imani just waved goodbye and kept it moving.

Chapter 12

Dave had been hearing Imani's name ring in the streets. She was often referred to as the goat or the plug. He couldn't believe the girl he knew at home was so ultra-powerful, demanding, and assertive in the streets in a game full of super ego men.

At home, Imani wouldn't talk business to Dave. he was used to that growing up with Caesar and Mama Ross.

To Dave Imani did everything right. She cooked, cleaned, and brought bags full of money home. most days Imani just played the ps4 with him wearing a t-shirt and no panties. She was his lover and friend.

"I missed you yo," Dave said playfully.

"I ain't your yo," Imani teased as she paused the game. She turned on her beats pill and Finao Love's "Down" blasted through. He was an artist out of Baltimore that they both loved. His music could get anybody in the mood.

Imani laid back on the bed and spread her legs into a V-shape inviting Dave into her paradise. Dave slipped his penis out with one hand and allowed it to rest on his thigh as he climbed on top of her. He parted her ocean with the head of his large member teasing her immensely. Imani's legs began to shake and cum dripped down her legs, and he didn't even penetrate yet. He wiped the juices from her inner thigh and glazed his dick with it slowly beating it. As the song entitled, he had to go down and taste it. Still stroking himself he feasted on Imani. His tongue quickly ran over the clit while randomly slurping her juices. He could tell by her moans and her digging her nails into his head he was doing great. Three minutes later he felt her body tense and her womanhood get warm so he dived his head in deeper. Shaking his head like he was having a seizure against the grain where she could feel his tongue, full lips, and facial hair. Just as he expected, she squirted all over his face. Dave never allowed her to catch her breath he already began digging in deep into her guts.

"Oh shit daddy," Imani moaned wrapping her legs around Dave's waist tighter.

"This my pussy?" Dave inquired.

Almost pausing for a second she answered, "yes" and dismissed the guilt from her.

Dave continued to give her his best moves before pausing their lovemaking session. "Will you marry me?"

Imani happily said, "yes."

Chapter 13

Imani and Dave had a simple wedding where the I dos and reception were all at the same place. Everyone was in attendance except Jodi and K.O. K.O. was sent away on business, but Jodi had no excuse. He just out right didn't show. It pained him to fake happy for Dave and Imani when he knows Caesar was so against their union.

That stuck out to Imani as she viewed the guest from behind a curtain. It's clear we are strictly business, not friends. He can't stand me. He's jealous that I took over. And now with my vows, I'm definitely not going anywhere, so Imani thought.

She decided to smile instead of letting that dampen her mood besides everything was beautiful. A large beautiful tent and flooring had been erected on the lawn where the reception was to be held. Upon arrival, guests were invited to enjoy a cocktail by the pool before the ceremony.

Mama Ross did all the inviting being that Imani was a loner and had no family, no friends, nobody that she allowed to get close to her.

Once all the guest arrived they found their seats around a custom made gazebo, waiting for, the bride- Imani to make her entrance.

The doors opened, and the curtain peeled back on the other side of the pool and Imani gracefully walked out. Her body embraced the Vera Wang mermaid dress laced and white and silver beading. She kept her veil short, reminiscent of the 1950's fashion. Her eyes only meeting with Dave, her soon to be husband.

The nuptial were pretty standard. If anybody should feel why these two shouldn't be wed, speak now or forever hold u piece blah blah blah. Nobody would dare object.

"You may now exchange the rings," the pastor informed.

Dave managed to slip passports out with the wedding band when it was time to place the band on Imani's finger. She snatched the passport like an eager kid awaiting to open a bag of chips. The crowd laughed. Inside the passport were tickets to Disney World Tokyo.

Dave knows me so well. I am a kid at heart and a jet setter so it would serve aa a fabulous honeymoon.

****

Its election day so all the kids were out of school and people were off from work. Imani could've done her civil duty and voted, but it wasn't a box that she could check that said let's try again next year.

Dave and Imani only been married for three months but Imani was already feeling regretful.

Dave hasn't done anything. He's right under my thumb like I want but it's me. It's me! I've tried fighting the urges and going against what feels normal to me, but I failed.

Imani

Imani had been sleeping with K.O. for a month now, and it was her new addiction. Dave's sex was good, but K.O.'s was better. He had a better stroke, but he was just as freaky as Dave They did everything from titty fucking to eating ass. She would squirt ten times in a row

They would meet at this bed and breakfast spot in Laurel, MD. Imani scanned the parking lot to see his car but to no avail. I must've beaten him here.

Imani walked to room 222 and slide the hotel key into the door. K.O. was already inside on the bed naked awaiting for her arrival to her surprise. She noticed his gun was close by.

The sight of his pretty, thick black dick always gets me wet. Imani instantly dropped to her knees. She loved sucking dick when aroused.

"Shit girl!" K.O. Moaned through clenched teeth. He was ready to cum but refused to so he forcefully pushed Imani off of him and flung her on the bed. K.O. grabbed a handful of Imani's hair with one hand while with the other he places her ankles by her head undressing her from the waist down.

It was pure heaven for Imani when he finally slid in and out.

"This big enough for you?" He asked.

"Yes daddy," Imani said arching her back in enjoyment.

K.O. flipped her over and held Imani deep into the mattress spreading her legs far apart ramming into her harder and harder causing her to squirt. He had her- hook, line, and sinker.

Chapter 14

The affair been going on for months and Imani's devoted husband was blissfully unaware.

Sometimes I look in the mirror and don't recognize myself. I've become extremely addicted to the money, power, and sex.

K.O. being the real nigga, he is he never faulted on the business side, and he never ratted out Imani to Dave. For that Imani bumped his pay way up. Out of all the secrets, this was the best and heaviest one. Depending upon the day sometimes she was sorry and other days it was like the lyrics to the song blasting on the car radio I ain't sorry nigga nah.

Imani cruised down the highway back to the usual spot- the bed and breakfast in Laurel, MD. Dave had graduated from Coppin with honors with a bachelor in mass communications. Dave and Imani went on a bae-cation (couples trip) two weeks ago to Cancun just to come back in town yesterday afternoon so that his foundation can host a charity basketball game in east Baltimore. Today Dave left to go to his internship with B.E.T. perfect excuse to call K.O. *I need my fix, I've been craving him.*

Stepping out of her car the hotel receptionist waved Imani down. 'Miss Imani they're just finishing up a maintenance order in your room so you can head up now. Kamari said he would return shortly."

"He was here?" Imani asked at the mention of K.O.'s birth name.

"Yes, but we couldn't let him in the room so he said he'll be back." The short and stout receptionist responded. This receptionist was there often when Imani and K.O. made an appearance. She was always friendly yet professional. The receptionist normally wore her wavy ginger colored hair in a curly ponytail. She appeared to be bi-racial and in her early twenty's.

Imani looked at the freckle face receptionist and shrugged before heading to the room. About thirty minutes later K.O. came staggering in reeking of Hennessey. Behind him were two females chuckling -one older and Caucasian, the other young and Cuban. Imani immediately felt uncomfortable. K.O. had never done something surprising like this. She pointed her gun towards the three of them, "Fuck is up?"

"Shh, relax baby " K.O. began slurring his words. "They just want to join the party. They're from outta town."

The older female chimed in, "My husband's the Mayor in Houston. He was smitten by you, and I must admit I've been wanting you ever since dear," Imani body evidently tensed up and her face struck confusion. "Don't worry hun. I'm not mad at you. We are swingers so he was free to do to you what I am about to do to you." The Caucasian women with dark hair and crow's feet around her ocean blue eyes walked over to Imani pushing the gun away and unbuttoning her blouse seductively. Taking one breast in at a time the Mayor's wife moaned while sucking Imani's ebony skin boobs. Imani felt K.O.'s hand undo her pants moving her panties to the side fingering her. When she moaned from K.O.'s heaven sent hands she began hearing slurping. Imani glanced over and saw the Cuban girl giving her best blow job. It immediately made Imani aroused and jealous at the same time so she leaned over and kissed K.O. passionately. The rest of the night was a sex-hazed blur.

Chapter 15

Dave had been outta town interning for B.E.T. for a few weeks now, and Imani could feel the distance. It wasn't the Miles affecting them either. It was his whole demeanor towards Imani as if she was the plaque.

This shit hurts deeply, and now I know for sure that I love him. I may have doubted myself with my feelings for him due to my actions, but I do I really do love him. So I had to stop sleeping with K.O. I don't think he cared one way or the other. As much fun I had with him my husband meant more. I gotta make things right with him when he returns.

The TV was on CNN, but Imani's back was turned to it. She was too busy in her thoughts and counting the money that she wanted to put in the retirement fund. Thirty thousand dollar in cash she counted by hand and sat it on the table when Dave stormed in.

"Hey baby," Imani said timidly since his attitude towards her has been less than pleasant lately. For the first time in their relationship, she didn't feel in control.

"Don't hey baby me" Dave spat with affirmed hostility. He looked at the money laying on the table, "what's this more money from popping ya pussy Infinity?"

"What?" Imani asked confused.

Dave cusped Imani's neck with his left hand," Now isn't the time to lie to me." He tossed a cd from his back pocket onto the floor than continued, "I've been sitting on this information for a while now. If this was hearsay, I would never bother you with it because your my wife and I trusted you but a hardcore sex tape of you, K.O, and the Mayor's wife is hard to deny."

Imani stood silently, completely frozen in place. "Why?" Dave asked yet Imani remained silent. "Speak bitch! " he barked.

Quivering where she stood Imani began, "I-I-I have been stripping and prostituting basically my entire life and before you, sex wasn't a fun option to a relationship it was a method of survival. I guess that's why I was never able to cum. You honestly put it on me and then all of a sudden I got curious about K.O." The tears began to flow freely down Imani's face. "It was no reason for me to have been curious. You were my king you were good to me, and I broke my vows to you with K.O. and I'm sorry. I did cut it off already," Imani hopes that had softened the blow.

Dave paced the floor unsympathetic or relieved but angrier, "what about the Mayor and his wife?"

"That was just money to me. I expanded your family's business to nightclub owners and prostitution. I asked the Mayor to keep the boys (police) away from our business affairs. In exchange, he wanted the cut of the profit and some pussy."

Dave flipped the table, being that it was glass it shattered into a million pieces cutting Imani's foot. She hopped away in agony lifting her pants leg to caress her foot." Baby please" she begged.

Dave grabbed her hair pulling it with every word he spoke, "Please what?! You've been lying from the beginning. Look at you! Pitiful now because you're caught. You said you had a twin come to find out it was you all along. My brother went to the club that night to find you and got killed, but there goes that tattoo on ya ankle that he spoke of!" He pointed to Imani's ankle, and she cried harder.

For years she had been putting bridal make up on her ankle to cover up her tattoo so he would never find out about her stripping. Even in the beginning when she went to Houston, Atlanta, and Vegas all in one week she disposed the heroin and also stripped. She didn't know how to do anything different than what she always has. Realizing the lengths that she had gone through to live a double life she was disgusted with herself.

Dave continued yelling, "my family business didn't need your expansion. We were living lavish before you. You were just being greedy! Its eight hundred thousand fucking dollars in cash stashed away, and you were still counting money when I walked in this bitch! All that talk about early retirement was bullshit. You're just another vain bitch addicted to designer clothes, flashy cars filled with greed, power, and lust. You are a low self-esteem classless bitch. You are the very type bitch my family warned me of, and I'm disgusted by you. He hawked spit in Imani's face and threw her to the ground. Walking to the front door, Dave said, "I'm divorcing you. I am so glad Jodi followed you and bugged that hotel so I could leave instead of spending my days with a hoe! But the way Jodi is in char-"

He was interrupted by the blaring television Breaking News Mayor and socialite of Houston dies of Aids tonight. Apparently, he's lives a double life of nymphomaniac playboy for some time now. With his numerous sex partners, that's how he contracted the deadly disease. The Mayor didn't find out until his cell count was too depleted for assistance with medication. He leaves behind three kids and a wife. The wife has also confirmed to have Aids as well.

Dave instantly dropped to the floor and sobbed, "you killed us all!"

Chapter 16

Going to the clinic to find their stats was one thing that will always be etched in their minds. Neither one of them wanted to be there, but they knew they had to. Of course, Dave still in his anger taunted Imani. "Bitch this is all your fault! Learn to be a lady and keep ya legs closed we wouldn't be knocking on death's door."

Dave threw plenty more insults in the waiting area causing other patience to turn their nose up at Imani. Imani ignored him. I deserve this. *I don't care about myself I just praying and hoping to God that Dave is spared. He's only twenty-two. He didn't begin to live nor have children.*

The nurse stepped out of silver steel plated door that led to the back and shouted, "Mr. And Mrs. Evans?"

"Not for long," Dave mumbled rising from his seat walking over to the nurse. Imani just shook her head in shame.

It wasn't long before they reached their perspective locations and was asked to give blood and urine sample. This clinic had a testing area in the facility so they would wait around for the results.

Knock, knock. A tall Arabian doctor came in with a crisp white jacket on and documents in hand. "You both have aids and not much longer to live. Your t counts..." Was the last thing that Imani heard the doctor say before fainting to the hard, shallow cold tile floors of the clinic.

Imani and Dave had been home together ever since the news with no calls, no visits, just them. Dave suggested it to be this way.

Several days had passed, and their home reeked with Imani and Dave's foul body odor. Neither of them talked to each other, ate, or showered. They were just there waiting to die. They didn't even bother to take medication that the doctors said would keep them comfortable. Why the hell would they? They were gonna die anyway.

The death I brought to us both I can't stand myself for. Just call me the grim reapers bitch. Imani thought. her eyes were red, big, and puffy from the endless tears she shed from guilt.

Dave had developed a dry cough and for his third day in a row, he was coughing uncontrollably. It even appeared his tongue was turning white and chaffing.

"Are you okay? Imani asked immediately regretting speaking to him. *I should never speak to him. I'm his enemy. I killed him.*

Dave got up slowly off the bed and walked over to the bedroom window peering out of the blinds. "No, I'm not okay! I'm dying. I can feel it. But most importantly I'm not okay with knowing whom I share my marriage bed with that lead to my demise. you've withheld information or lied since I met you. you know everything about me! Yet you're a stranger to me. I'll be okay once I know the real you."

Chapter 17

April 1997

The thunder crackled against the window pane. Imani was eight years old home alone for a fifth straight day. She survived off of chips, oodles the noodles, and tap water in a studio apartment. However today the water stopped running, and the noodles and chips were gone. She was forced to drink the toilet water. If she had to poop or pee, she had to do it in the bath tub to keep the toilet clean or what can be considered clean enough to drink.

Her mother often disappeared for days at a time chasing her drug habit. Yet Imani felt like she had it better than most kids she knew. She always had a roof over her head and clothes on her back even if they were outdated or too small.

Imani sat on the bed playing I declare war to pass the time trying to ignore the rumbling sounds in her tummy from hunger and the rumbling sounds of thunder and lightning from the Storm. The Storm was getting so loud it began to scare her when suddenly the doorknob forcefully turned. Her mother stumbled in the apartment with a tall bald head dark-skinned man with bulging eyes following closely behind.

"Hey, kiddo," Imani's mom said smiling. She looked as if she hadn't showered or combed her hair in days.

her face, and she wanted to stop, but mom said do what he says. That echoed in her head as Mr. E's penis ripped her eight-year-old virgin flesh. He stroked as if she was used to being penetrated. She was tighter than he ever experienced and he was overwhelmingly excited and rough against Imani's frail adolescent body. His body finally tensed and jerked, and he lazily removed himself from Imani.

She vomited at the foul act that just took place. she held it in for as long as she could. Mr. E didn't help he lay like a baby on the bathroom floor preparing for sleep.

Imani cried uncontrollably sliding off the bathroom sink being careful to step over him to get to her mother. She could barely walk. The pain was excruciating. Sharp pains ran through her body with each step she took. Her body was about to give out on me, but she finally made it to her mother whom was on the bed.

Catherine held Imani and rocked her. Imani buried her face in her mom's bosom hoping her stench would overcome the smell of sex, blood, sweat, and semen.

Chapter 18

August 1997

Imani wished this was the first and last time that occurred with Mr. E but it wasn't. And with each foul back shot he gave Imani her hatred for her mother grew. Catherine never saved her. She actually pimped her own daughter out and never shed a tear about it again. As long as Mr. E paid their rent, furnished the apartment, and kept Catherine high Imani was his for the taking.

On this particular August night, Imani saw the knob turning, and her stomach dropped. She just knew it was Mr. E. To her surprise it was her mother all alone.

"Hey kiddo" Catherine greeted Imani as always when she resurfaced. Imani said nothing. Catherine sat on the floor and began to tie herself off. At that pivotal moment, Imani knew her mom would never save her. She wasn't even the same. She changed for the worst. Catherine never did drugs in front of Imani.

Catherine began to nod out, and the angrier Imani grew. "Do you even love me?!" Imani screamed. Her mother never replied she was in a deep high. The non-response made Imani's blood boil.

With flashbacks of Mr. body on top of hers and her mother's failure to be a mom, Imani jabbed the extra needle into Catherine's arm pushing all the ingredients in. Scared of what she did, Imani quickly got any trace of her existence out of the apartment and ran to the man who was rumored to be her father.

Later Imani had heard her mom had been found dead. The police ruled it an overdose.

Chapter 19

May 2001

The man rumored to be Imani's father name was Levi. Levi took Imani in four years ago on that night and never asked any questions.

Since Imani didn't have any next of kin, he felt obligated to let her stay without hesitation. Imani had imagined the rough patch in her life had died with her mother. But she was wrong.

Every time she tried to get close to Levi he'd push her away. He only would say hi and bye for the first two years. He'd never take me shopping. She'd only get hand me downs from the many women he was sleeping with. Imani often felt just as alone as she did when she was in the studio apartment waiting for my mom to get off her high.

Alicia keys - diary blared through the radio speakers in Imani's bedroom. She laid on the bed in only a size A bra and some gym shorts focusing on nothing but the ceiling.

Suddenly Levi walked in with a woman and a young girl who was around Imani's age. "Imani this is Ms. Yvette, and this is Taylor." Levi introduced them to Imani with a cigarette hanging from his purple lips.

Imani didn't speak or move. Last time a parent of mine introduced me to someone my life got worse. I am in no mood to meet anyone.

"Girl you better speak to my daughter and her mama" Levi demanded of Imani.

Imani waved due to her throat being too dry to verbally communicate. On the inside, she was dying. I lived with him for four years, and he never claimed me as he did all of my life. I'd never have a spot in his life or heart. I was simply a tenant.

The more reality sat in, the more Imani pierced a hole through the girl Taylor's skull with her eyes. Taylor was a beautiful girl. Her hair was in a neat bun, her Baby Phat outfit did her tall model figure well. The 14 carat gold name earrings and matching necklace shined brightly, and her nails polished pink. Imani envied her. Not only did she have Levi's heart and attention but she had style too. Taylor had swag before it was even thought of.

"Levi were gonna go," Mrs. Yvette said feeling the tension. They left out the front door, and Levi went into his room where Imani followed.

"Why don't you consider me a daughter?" Imani asked bluntly with tear filled eyes.

"Because you were never meant to be mine. Your mother was a mistake. And hell I was one of many men."

"So your calling my mama a ho?" Imani asked knowing the answer already. She knew her mama had an addiction way before she came into the picture and got her fix by spreading her legs. Imani wished she could defend her mother whole heartedly but fuck that bitch too, she thought.

" she damn sure wasn't a saint. Just a drug using a ho with a great body. I'm reminded every time I look at you" Levi said tracing y shape with his lingering eyes. Imani hips, thighs, and booty resembled an older woman thanks to my mom.

Levi grabbed my hand and pulled Imani closer to him. She could feel his manhood rise "You want to call me daddy?" He swiped his finger against her clit through the gym shorts.

Imani smiled and closed her eyes and with all the strength she could muster she kicked him hard in the nuts. He doubled over in pain. Quickly Imani took the dresser lamp and broke it across Levi's head. He was out cold. Imani took all of the cash out of his wallet, packed her clothes, and roamed the streets.

Hours later Imani decided to stay at a cheap motel in only thinking of getting through tonight. She was approached with two problems, however. Imani wasn't eighteen years old nor did she have ID to book a room.

Imani sat outside the hotel pondering her next move. There was a white guy standing in front alongside her, smoking a cigar, cutting his eye at her ever so often.

"What?!" Imani asked rudely.

"You look deep in thought!" The guy snapped back.

"I'm deep in minding my own business!" Imani shouted.

"No need to be rude but do you need help?" The guy asked. Imani stayed silent. "I can help. My name is Bob" he extended his hand. Imani was hesitant to shake it back. "What do you need?" Bob asked.

"Someone to book the room for me. I have my own money," Imani reluctantly answered waving around the money that she stole out of Levi's wallet.

"How much is that?"

"Sixty"

Bob started scratching his chin, "That's only enough for two nights. What's ya plan afterwards? How are you gonna eat?"

"I'm just living for today."

Bob walked inside the hotel and Imani followed. "Let me get a room for one-night charge it to my card please," Bob stated to the hotel associate. The clerk handed him a room key, and both Imani and Bob went into the direction where the room would be.

"Here's ya money sir," Imani said extending thirty dollars to him.

"No keep it" Bob answered unlocking the motel room door.

Imani had anticipated this Bob man to leave her to her own devices, but he sat in the recliner that was pressed against the corner wall of the motel room. "Is there something I can help you with?" Imani placed her hands on her hips.

"I just want to make sure you're okay. You won't survive off of sixty dollars" Bob schooled the young Imani plainly.

"So what you want to take care of me in exchange for pussy," Imani said extremely agitated.

"What are you anywhere from twelve to fifteen? And the fact that you said that means you've already been tried. Instead of letting a man have power over ya pussy you can use ya pussy as power." Bob paused for a moment studying Imani's face. Her wheels were turning. Bob leaned back in the recliner. "I got a strip club, and we do private parties. Anything goes. you're a gorgeous girl, and you got a body. Clearly, you're are not a virgin anymore so use yours to survive. After that, you can be a doctor or sum shit."

That same night Imani agreed to his offer by learning to suck dick. Imani stripped for and lived with Bob till she was twenty-one.

Chapter 20

June 2001

Imani made her way to the Pataspaco Flea Market which was on the brinks of Cherry Hill. Cherry Hill was essentially Baltimore's last waterfront community. It was broken up into sections- port Covington and Westport. The nature of the neighborhood was an overpopulated sector for public housing with an onslaught of decent business- car washes, McDonald's, roses, banks, long john silvers, liquor stores, and hospitals just to name a few. Not to mention plenty of bus lines and light rail stations nearby while being minutes away from downtown to club or get to a greyhound station to flee Baltimore.

Imani stepped off the bus adjusting her book bag on her back. The humidity casted over Imani as she made her way through the neighborhood. It was summertime so everyone was outside. There were kids scattered about for Miles running around playing. In the distance, you could hear the tunes of an ice cream truck.

Various men stood outside talking their shit while others just came back from the store stocking up on plenty liquor, cigarettes, and Dutch masters.

During the walk, Imani continued to observe the sights and sounds of the neighborhood she was in. Even though every hood in Baltimore was different, it was genuinely the same. Some females were outside braiding hair while others argued with a boyfriend. The rest was trying to get a boyfriend. Imani stepped over various people emptying the gut of the blunt onto the street.

"My bad shorty," a guy said to Imani who was trying to prepare his blunt. Imani flashed a smile and kept in stride. Every two houses there was a different sound. All the summers hits roared from house and car speakers in passing. Ushers you remind me, hit em up style, to 112's Peaches and cream roared. Imai began to nod to whatever she heard next on the way to her destination.

"About three kids… " Imani recited the lyrics to a DMX song that played in the distance. She loved the collab with the Baltimore native. She didn't care if the song was old or not.

"You like that song huh shorty?" A guy wearing a white beater, denim shorts and a du-rag asked.

"So what if I do" Imani responded rudely.

"I don't want no trouble sweetheart. Your just so pretty" the guy stated.

"Thanks," Imani said unimpressed.

"Where you going?"

"To the flea market."

"That figures! What you plan on getting?" The guy asked

"I haven't decided yet," Imani said picking up her pace.

"Dang sweetheart I can't walk with you?" The guy frowned his face.

"No!" Imani said leaving the man where he stood.

The flea market in Baltimore is a huge space for bulk items for low prices through vendors. Imani didn't have much money being with Bob. She spent most on food and bus fare. She needed a few things. What she could buy she would, what she couldn't, she would steal. She already had that set in her head.

Imani zipped through the market coming across various tables, shops, and vendors. She stocked up on bras and panties, toiletries, and smell goods. After excessing her damage, she had only enough money left for bus fare for another day. That wasn't gonna stop her shine, though. Imani wanted to look at some female clothing before heading out. She would just have to use her five finger discount.

She approached a table that had piles of neatly folded graphic tees scattered around. The shirts were an assortment of colors, Some name brand and some not. The worker never really paid Imani any attention. She was too swamped with her paying, returning customers. Every time the worker parted her back to Imani, she would grab a shirt quickly placing it in her book bag which dangled loosely off her arms and was halfway unzipped. Imani pulled this off about six more times before the worker focused on her.

"May I help you?"

"No, I'm still deciding" Imani answered pretending to be in deep thought about choosing between two shirts.

"I honestly think the pink one would better suit you," the worker stated beginning her sales pitch. "These shirts are two for fifteen, and they are fit to size. They will not shrink after you wash them."

"Okay that's good to know," Imani said pretending to still browse.

"So do you think you want the pink one or both? It's only two for fifteen" the worker pushed.

Imani didn't say a word. She purposely paused pretending to be in deep thought. "Maybe next time" she finally responded and quickly turned to leave.

Once she turned she seen a familiar face inches away from where she stood. The tall, skinny, modelesque pretty face girl clung onto Levi's arms. The girl was Taylor. She and her mother gazed Levi in the face as he talked. It seemed they clung on his every word. To someone outside looking in, they seemed like the perfect black family. This infuriated Imani.

Taylor noticed a girl staring at her with hateful eyes. Once she recognized the girl, she tapped Levi on the shoulder trying to get his attention. He was browsing some watches.

"What?!" Imani asked aggressively. She couldn't stand Taylor and couldn't imagine why the girl would even look in her direction.

Levi turned around instantly at the sound of Imani's voice "Step behind me Taylor please," He began motioning for Taylor to move.

"Yeah hide behind ya punk ass child molesting ass daddy!" Imani spat.

"What?" Taylor asked confused.

"Watch ya mouth!" Levi warned Imani.

"Don't believe her," the mother spoke to Taylor caressing her head.

"Shut up bitch!" Imani said with venom in her veins. Why the fuck is she talking.

"Don't talk to my mama like that," Taylor stepped alongside Levi.

"Or what?" Imani said taking one step.

"You're just jealous!"

"Jealous?" Imani acted as if she didn't know the term.

"Yes jealous that I have a daddy, and you don't. He tried to help you but your so mean and ungrateful. Now look at you standing here looking a mess" Taylor said lighting a match to an already lit flame.

Imani was super surprised act the sudden boldness of Taylor. She seemed so meek. Imani forgot that she was a sassy temperamental pre-teen just like her. Nevertheless, the hatred she had in her heart for Levi and his perfect family wouldn't let her take this lying down. In a blind rage, she attacked Taylor landing a few good punches before Levi pushed Imani off of Taylor. Taylor's mom dragged Imani by the hair and Imani kicked the woman in her gut causing her to stumble back in pain. The shoppers nearby let out a series of gasps as the fight continued. Imani kept punching hitting both

Levi and Taylor. Imani could feel the tears stream down her face. Imani's shopping bags flew everywhere. The stolen merchandise had fallen out of her book bag which she forgot to zip 'em back up. Security came and ceased the violence.

"What the hell is going?" The security guard asked restraining Imani.

"This girl attacked us!" Taylor's mom said slowly getting up holding her stomach.

"For what?" The guard asked Imani remained silent.

"Cause my dad isn't my father," Taylor threw salt on the wound.

"Yes, he is my father!" Imani screamed.

"Sir what the heck is going on here?" The security asked getting annoyed dealing with the three childish women. "Is this your daughter or not?"

A devilish grin escaped Levi before he answered, "Yes she is. She has been a troubled child for a while. Always very abusive and she ran away from home. She knocked me out with a lamp. Look here I had to get stitches" Levi pointed to the back of his head.

"And it looks like she was in here stealing," Taylor's mom said pointing to the merchandise spread across their feet.

"I just don't know what I can do anymore" Levi should have won an Oscar. He compelled the security guard as if he was a great father to Imani with his tone and facial expressions.

"Would you like to press charges? Maybe sometime in baby bookings would straighten her out." The guard suggested.

Levi wanted something done to her. He figured maybe she'll get her ass beat in bookings for all the trouble she caused him and his family. Once the court papers came, he would never appear in court. He didn't want no parts of her. He knew the charges would be dropped if he didn't show up for court but with Imani being a minor she would be a ward of the state in a group home. Either way, she would be out of his hair.

"I guess so. What can I do?" Levi said pretending to be conflicted. Taylor and the mom watched it play out. They always allowed Levi to lead.

"So you pressing charges now nigga?!" Imani asked getting angrier in the guard's strong hold.

"Wait for the squad car. Okay now, nothing to see here people!" The guard spoke hauling the lurking crowd away and taking Imani away.

Imani sat in the back of the police car and watched helplessly as Levi gave the cop a false report. All she ever wanted was for Levi to claim her and when he finally did it was with ill intent. Imani never learned the saying once someone shows you who they are the first time believe them. But boy was she feeling it. Levi gave his final statements and told the officer to have a nice day. When he was sure the officer wasn't looking Levi stared at Imani with a sinister grin and blew her kiss. If Imani wasn't handcuffed, she would've given him the middle finger.

At the precinct, it was empty. It was just her and the officer that brought her in. He handcuffed Imani to a bench and began to type up the report.

"Don't I get a phone call or something?' Imani asked.

"What you know about getting a phone call?" The cop raised an eyebrow. "You've been in jail before?"

"Nope. I watched a lot of New York Undercover," Imani said shifting herself on the bench. The handcuffs were hurting her wrist. "Can you take these off they hurt!"

"Okay little girl, one phone call, and you can come out the cuffs just promise to behave yaself. This is supposed to be easy overtime for me."

"Sure," Imani said relieved to be getting the cuffs off.

The cop walked her over to the phone, and she dialed Bob's number. He was at the club doing inventory as usual."

"This is Bob" he answered.

"It's Imani I'm down the precinct. They got me on assault and theft, and some whole other shit come get me."

"What?!" Bob was vexed.

"Please come get me it wasn't my fault my dad pulled some snake shit" Imani's voice cracked but she held in her cry. She didn't want to be in jail 'cause she knew the moment they ran her name she would be in foster care. She didn't have any family. She wasn't going to school, and she lived under the radar for so long she figured a heap of questions would follow.

"Which precinct?" Bob asked.

"The one closest to the flea market," Bob hung up. Imani turned to sit back on the bench.

"Everything squared away?" The cop asked.

"Why do you care? You're on Levi's side ain't you," Imani hissed.

"Actually, I don't give a fuck. I'm just making conversation. I'm on nobody side," he answered stretching out in his chair. "I do believe I get tired of seeing more and more kids during bookings."

"Aww what you got a little modern day I have a dream speech for kids like me," Imani taunted.

"That's what's wrong with y'all kids. Got all that mouth but don't know shit. Why you gotta get all smart. Why can't I just be a nice guy wanting more for the next generation.?"

Imani sat up causing her boobs to sit a little perkier. "I don't know any nice guys. All guys usually do some evil."

"Is that right?" He unintentionally scanned over her body. He never looked at a girl younger than him. But her beauty stuck him on this summer day. His longtime girlfriend was a devout Christian and haven't been giving up the goods. On a daily basis, it was a struggle to keep himself to himself.

Imani chuckled when she caught his glances. "If I seen it once I've seen it twice." The cop swallowed hard. "What's ya name?"

"Alex smith."

"Alex, I'm Imani. Look can you help me out, please. Let me go with my uncle and drop the charges. Get rid of the report I promise to stay out the precinct and the flea market. I promise my uncle will see to it that I'm behaved. I just don't need to go down this path. Your right my generation needs to do better," Imani was playing the game the way Bob taught her to. She was still a rookie but to save her own ass she had to become a pro at this moment.

"That's what they all say," Alex said fixing his pants. It was something starting to bulge.

Imani walked over to him seductively. She grabbed his hands and placed it on her chest. "I'm serious," she said. Imani grabbed his belt and unbuckled it causing his uniform pants to sag. She pulled his short, thick dick out of his black boxers.

"Wait," Alex moaned. He got up and went into a spare room and fondled with some equipment. He came back out with a cassette in his hand. "There will be no precinct footage of this!" He said out loud and made his way back to his chair. He got comfortable in the seat and allowed Imani to give him the best five-minute head of his life. It didn't take much for him to cum since he was sex deprived. When he squirted in her mouth, she let it drop to the front and caught it again. The sight of this made him rock hard moments later. He was ready for round two. She spit on his manhood and went to work.

Alex just managed to get his second nut off when Bob arrived. Bob noticed Alex fixing his pants and Imani leaning over the trash can spitting. "I'm here for her my niece."

"Oh okay, sir. Take her the charges been dropped she just can't ever go to the flea market." Alex said.

"No problem," Bob said leading the way out the precinct. Imani followed. She only looked back once to blow Alex a kiss.

"I've seen you handle yaself, baby girl," Bob said getting in the truck.

"Yea," Imani answered nonchalantly.

"Look I don't want to keep picking you up from jail so cut all the crap out. Besides stealing is just unacceptable! And from now on you tell me where you are going!" Bob scolded.

"Okay Bob," Imani answered as they drove away.

Chapter 21

July 2001

Imani had been living with Bob for months at this point. All she had ever been booked for was private shows. Private shows never entailed dancing of any kind. It was just straight up- face down, ass up type of fucking. So imagine Imani's surprise when Bob finally pulled her ass to the strip club.

"Tonight's the night!" Bob said excitedly clutching at Imani's shoulders. Bob used Imani's shoulders as a way to snake through the crowded club to get to the dressing room.

Imani felt all of the nervousness fall to the pit of her stomach with each step she took. The DJ was blazing the hottest of tunes. By the looks of things, the club was more than generous with talent and entertainment for tonight. The bar was stocked with gallons of liquor. The club itself was dim with flashing strobe lights with a scent of sweat, ass, perfume, liquor, and weed underlying it.

Bob and Imani finally made it to the dressing area. The few girls that were there paused what they were doing and looked in Imani's and Bob's direction when the door creaked open. Once they noticed it was just then Bob, they quickly went back to their routine.

Most of the girls were already on the floor so the dressing room was fairly empty. Imani could breathe easy momentarily.

"I am going to go to the office and do the books. Get dressed and when you hear the name Infinity go to the stage." Bob said with his groin pressed up against Imani's lower body. It wasn't sexual so Imani did not mind. She knew he was only that close to her to kill the anxiousness that dwelled within her about her first night.

"How did you come up with Infinity?" Imani asked prolonging Bob's departure.

"It was easy. The real power within that you exude is to infinity and beyond. You're rare and timeless woman. If only you'd tap into it " Bob walked away letting his words fall into her spirit.

Imani by age wasn't a woman yet, and all the bullshit she went through with her parents didn't make her feel as precious as Bob had hyped her to be. Imani walked up to an empty vanity and removed a small backpack from her back and sat it down. She stripped down out of her new crisp Air Forces, baby doll tee, and denim jeans. Her bra and underwear soon disappeared as she removed a sexy see through school girl outfit that Bob had picked out. he played on her age and youthful face. Imani oiled her entire body down before putting the outfit on.

"I can do this," Imani said out loud to nobody in particular.

"Yes, you can, girl. Get this money and block this place out ya head when you're done" one of the dancers said idly walking past. The dancer was pretty with chinky eyes and long black hair.

"That's Adore! " yet another dancer chimed in walking up behind Imani. The dancer just stared awaiting for her to say something. Imani didn't say anything. "Hi my name is Satin" she introduced herself to Imani.

"Infinity" Imani answered glancing at her own reflection in the mirror figuring the girl gave a stage name so she didn't want to be too formal.

"The girl that spoke the first time is Adore. She is real saditty. She just here to pay her way through college. That's it that is all. She literally does her three minutes on stage, get her lap dances in and bounces out. Adore isn't down for the extra."

Imani didn't like the way Satin said extra because she knew what extra was code for. Well, she wouldn't like me then, Imani thought. All she had been doing is extra stuff. This is her first night in the club to actually dance.

"So it's three minutes you say?" Imani asked Satin.

"First time?"

Imani just nodded.

Satin let out a sigh, "Yeah girl its only three minutes. Get ready for the friendly party goer to be like baby this, baby that," Satin did her best deep manly voice impersonation while changing to a drunken slur, "Be on the lookout for the drunken fool that's saying aye bitch or let's go hoe."

Imani allowed Satin's expertise to set in.

"Come on let me do your make-up and let's make this money," Satin said as she pushed Imani down in the chair and opened a brand new makeup palette. One of the strippers left it lying around. Imani never protested. She was simply glad someone could help. Bob was a man and he didn't know how to apply make-up and Imani was too young and too poor to even buy make-up to experiment with. Hell, she just got her period six months ago.

Satin gave Imani a natural look but highlighted her face to create the appeal of a sexy woman. This was it! It was no more stalling with small talk and make-up.

Imani's heart was pounding, her stomach in knots and hands were sweaty. Damn Imani shake it off. it ain't no worse than what you've already done.

Detecting Imani's hesitation Satin cusped her chin. "You need something to take the edge off?" Imani didn't reply, and she watched Satin walk over to a locker and retrieved a half folded ten-dollar bill. When she peeled it, white flurries went into the air.

Imani was immediately disgusted. She saw what hard drugs can do to a person first hand thanks to her mother, Catherine. As much as she would love for her nightmares to clear her head, that wouldn't be the answer. She vowed to herself to never try it.

Satin waved the bill in front of Imani's face. Imani shook her hands violently suggesting no. "I don't get down like that."

Satin raised an eyebrow but didn't make a big deal out of it. "Fuck it more for me than!" She lowered her head running her nose across the bill sniffing the substance hard. Once she was finished, she tucked the bill with the ones that were already in her crotch while gently wiped away any evidence from her nose or face. Satin held her head up for a few minutes trying to prevent her nose from running yet, in turn, making her throat burn. "Let's go!" she said making hurried steps. Imani followed behind her walking through the crowd.

Imani felt multiple hands touch her ass, but she ignored it. She scanned the room nervously for Bob but to no luck.

There were all types of men there- young, old, black, white, Hispanic, rich, and poor. It was one female in the room that wasn't an employee.

"It's dykes in here too?" Imani asked.

"Girl everyone is a trick" Satin replied to Imani raising her pitch to drown out the loud music. She suddenly licked her lips, bite her index finger, and smiled at a young man across the room. He winked at her.

It was about several others occupying the space that the young man was in. Satin pulled Imani by the wrist trying to help make Imani some money.

"What's up daddy?" Satin asked the young man.

"Do you even have to ask?" The young man answered the question with a question. He jokingly looked down at his crouch.

Satin laughed, "Anyways Ryan this is Infinity. Infinity meet Ryan."

"Wassup," Ryan said. Imani met it back with a sufficient head nod. Ryan was fine. He was tall and skinny, brown skin, with a Diamond stud in his ear.

The guy next to him waved some singles in Imani's direction signaling for a dance. Imani nervously obliged. She suppressed Imani for tonight and let Infinity build a name.

Satin and Imani took turns hoping from lap to lap from all the patron's that surrounded the area Ryan was in. The one sitting closest to Ryan was named Belly. He was named this due to it being the largest thing on him. At 6'1" 210 pounds, he was easy on the eyes. He just had a big stomach from all the beer he consumed daily. Belly was the middle child of his four siblings who were in attendance in the club tonight as well.

Mack- the oldest, wore a black shirt with an orioles fitted cap. His pants hung low off of his ass even when sitting down. The pants were cuffed over a pair of Filas. He eagerly the ones that he won at a dice game earlier that day.

Rico- the cutest brother of them all, was the youngest. He wore his hair cut low in a short bush, exposing his pretty curl pattern. You would never find him with a hair out of place. He was sitting next to the twins whom he shared the same green eyes with.

Melo and Melanie. Melo the male twin was always cool and calm. Often he stayed to himself. He had a cinnamon complexion that illuminated his green eyes. Their sister Melanie aka Mel was the outgoing twin.

Satin no matter what always made her way back to Ryan. She gave him more intimate touches than the rest of the tricks. Occasionally, Imani would see Satin caressing his ears and running her hands through his long braids. Imani assumed Ryan was hers. although she made eye contact with Ryan ever so often, she was careful not to for too long. She knew women were Territorial and didn't want the drama.

"Please welcome to the stage Adore!" The DJ announced loudly. The hip hop beats instantly faded to black and R. Kelly's "Your Body" began to play.

Adore swayed seductively while everyone in the club did the same getting into a groove. The song was taking them back.

Imani was giving Belly a lap dance when he pulled a baggie out of his back pocket. He wrapped his arms around Imani showing her the baggie and pulling her closer to him.

"Are you trying get lifted?" Belly asked.

"Naw I'm good," Imani said pushing the baggie out of her view.

"You smoke?" Mel asked. Imani's eyebrows raised as if to say smoke what. Mel made eye contact with Ryan which made Imani look at him as well. Ryan held up a blunt. "He's always holding. Put it in the air man," Mel coaxed.

Ryan lit it and took his two puffs and passed it to Imani. Why not Imani thought and let the weed settle into her lungs.

She only coughed a little. Imani passed the blunt to Mel and walked back over to Ryan since Satin left him alone to be with Belly to share the white contents of the baggie.

Imani and Ryan shook their heads. They didn't want to stand in judgment of them, they just didn't get down like that.

Scanning around the room Imani could make out a shadow that looked like Bob. She was thinking of walking over to him but...

"Welcome to the stage a fresh face. She's beautiful and any man's school yard fantasy. Welcome, Infinity!" The DJ said. The beat to back that ass up roared through the club and the dancers scattered around the club got hype waiting for the bass to drop.

Imani swallowed her own saliva heard and sexily snaked her way through the crowd to the stage. Once on stage she purposely bent down in a downward dog position causing the already short school girl skirt to expose her phat ass. She stayed in that position long enough to wipe off the prior stripper's juices from the pole.

"Fucking dance girl!" A random man said in a stern voice.

Imani began to work the pole. She ran her ass crack up and down the pole. Then she did some tricks she learned from watching B.E.T. uncut. the stage was hot under the lights causing her to sweat. Imani took off her shirt and threw it into the crowd. She swung around the pole in a series of tricks. Imani ended the song in a split. The crowd went crazy, and the stage was covered in bills. She seductively crawled around retrieving all the money.

Bob walked over helping Imani off the stage. Adore gave her a round of applause as she sat on some chubby niggas lap. " was that so bad?" Bob asked Imani sitting her on a bar stool.

"Guess not" Imani stated starting to feel the effects of the weed.

"Bartender give the young lady a cranberry and vodka and give me a beer," Bob yelled over his shoulders. he then swooped the money out of Imani's hands. She didn't make a fuss.

Imani watched him count it all twice and then peeled off some stuffing it into his pocket giving the rest of it back to Imani. His cut as previously discussed. Sixty- forty Imani thought.

Drinks were sitting in front of them when a sweaty Satin came in between them. "Hey, Bob do you mind if me and Infinity get breakfast afterwards."

"Sure don't," Bob answered holding his hand out. Satin sucked her teeth but gave him his cut. With that how walked away with his beer in hand.

"You did that!" Satin complimented Imani slapping her thigh.

"Thanks, girl I was nervous as I don't know what."

"Fuck all that cause I couldn't tell," Satin said excitedly stealing some of Imani's drink while slapping Imani on the thigh again.

This girl is real friendly. Imani didn't want to bark about a sip of her alcohol. The girl had been by her side all night being nothing but supportive. This is what friendship is I guess Imani thought. They danced until the club closed.

A group of dancers rushed out the club now dressed in regular clothes Imani and Satin included. There were still some tricks outside trying their hardest to get some pussy.

"Bye ladies" Ryan yelled out of his Buick window. It wasn't a flashy car by a long shot. A smile crept on Satin's face.

"So who is that?" Imani was being nosey.

"That's just my supplier!" Satin stated not divulging much more information than that. A van pulled up curbside next to Imani and Satin. The windows rolled down, and a bottle came flying out.

Satin and Imani immediately jumped aside and the bottle hit Adore square in the head. She was chatting with the same chubby guy from earlier. Actually, she was declining his offer to be in his bed tonight.

"Darlene what the fuck are you doing?!" The chubby guy asked. Adore was out cold on the cement, blood leaking into the gutter.

Darlene stepped out of the minivan. She was extremely short and not attractive. "I could be asking you the same thing!"

"I'm outchere just enjoying the city, and you come down here on ya bullshit," the chubby man said

"Paul I'm not stupid. You're out looking for pussy. I'm so tired of ya little dick ass cheating on me while I'm home with the kids" Darlene ranted.

"Where are the kids?"

"Man fuck you and them kids!" Darlene snapped before retrieving a gun out of the bathrobe she wore. It was so much venom behind her eyes it scared chubby Paul more than the gun. She emptied the entire clip on Paul. Realizing what she done, she got back in the minivan and sped away.

Everyone on the scene made hurried steps away. Yet police were coming from every corner. "My truck is this way!" Satin said leading the way damn near sprinting. A cop car cut her off.

"Good evening ladies," he said getting out of the car just then two more dancers walked in their direction and immediately wished they hadn't.

The young fresh faced Caucasian male officer screamed rookie. He thought it would be easier to talk to a group of females than it would be males. unknown to him females were sometimes worse than men and lived by the same code. "do you guys have a clue to what happened in front the club?"

"Don't know nothing about no club," Satin immediately spoke. The officer scanned the eyes of the other ladies.

"Ain't seen shit" a dancer replied.

"Don't know shit" the other dancer picked up.

"Ain't you ever heard of stop snitching!" Imani added trying to follow suit. Ordinarily, any other female would have got beat on for making such a snide comment like that. They knew Imani was new, young and green to the shit so they all fell out in laughter walking away leaving the rookie cop stuck on stupid.

Chapter 22

The same night

In the car, Imani had expressed feeling bad leaving Adore to bleed out on the cold concrete of Baltimore. Not even giving her justice. They couldn't give her her life back, but at least we could've done something, Imani thought

"Youngin you better get tough skin. You will see some shit and do some shit ever so often in this business. Ain't nobody in that damn club friends." Satin said smoking a cigarette. Quiet as kept Satin hated seeing fights and dead bodies. She had manipulated enough things to happen in front of her and always needed something to take the edge off.

Imani couldn't get past the nobody in the club is friends comment. Than what the fuck are we? She thought. Imani let the thought fall to the waist side as they went into Valentino's to get some grub. It wasn't breakfast time, but not much stayed open past two in the morning in Baltimore.

Over a meal, Satin gave the low down on all the strippers in the club. It was about twenty of them. Imani made twenty-one. There was Satin, Adore, Pebbles and Peaches (the two girls who spoke to the rookie cop), Duchess, Sapphire, Lyric, London, China, Shyne, Angel, Whynetta, Keke, Indigo, Tera, Mira, Lacey, Storm, Diamond, and Chocolate.

"Whynetta is nosey as hell. Bob brought her in personally. I don't think they ever fucked, but I wouldn't run it past him. He does get down with the help sometimes" Satin spoke. Imani continued to stuff her face. She didn't feel one way or the other about what Bob did or didn't do. "Oh, Tera and Mira are sisters. Shyne and Keke are straight up thieves. Duchess really thinks she a queen but makes the least money there. Niggas ain't checking for her. She be on a trick like what's up daddy, and they be like not you bitch." Satin chuckled. She sipped on her water placing her index finger up as a signal to wait. As she placed the cup back on the table, she continued, "Chocolate is my bitch! Once again nobody in there is friends but she's my bitch. Everyone else is just tricking getting money. No shame in the game."

Satin looked down, and her meal was gone. Imani had a spoonful left of her meal. "Hope you don't think you will be knowing my story," Imani stated.

Satin raised an eyebrow and smiled "the truth always exposes itself. Your story will eventually be told." With that, she left a bill on the table. "It's my treat!" Satin said walking out of the restaurant.

****

Satin gave a lame, bogus ass story about being too tired to drive Imani back to Bob's house. They went inside her low income apartment. It was comfortably laid out.

The furniture was all white. She had Satin material everything.

114

"Make yaself comfortable," Satin said as she disappeared into the bedroom.

When she came back out, she wore only a thong.

"Girl what the- " Imani tried to complain but Satin cut her short.

"Bitch you seen my pussy all night don't trip," Satin said sitting on the floor cutting lines of dope on her coffee table. Imani watched silently as she snorted each line. "How long you and Bob been knowing each other?"

"Didn't I say you wasn't knowing my story" Imani answered coolly. She began to walk around looking at the various paintings on the wall.

"Fuck it, we don't have to talk. I would rather put you up on game anyway," Satin said walking up behind Imani leaning against her.

Imani could feel Satin's breast pressing against the small of her back. She felt as soft as her name implied. Satin began kissing Imani on her neck and made her way down to the dimples in her back. She turned Imani around to face her.

"Don't!" Imani pleaded.

"But I want to," Satin said tracing Imani's nipples through the baby doll tee. Imani still didn't budge. "Look cons gonna be males and females so get used to it!" Satin grew frustrated.

"So are you paying me?" Imani asked, and Satin smiled.

"That's a smart girl. Cash for ass" Satin led Imani by the hand to the couch. Taking off her shoes and jeans rubbing from her feet to her inner thigh. Planting gentle kisses everywhere in between.

Imani was getting comfortable when Satin stopped abruptly and went into the bedroom. Seconds later she darted out with money and a strap on. Satin flipped Imani over her stomach and began pounding like a savage with the dildo. She clutched Imani's wide, sexy baby making hips. Imani buried her face in the pillow while Satin rhythmically stroked.

"Hold that pose bitch!" Satin said still stroking grabbing Imani's waist with one hand, fingering Imani's clit with the other

As time went, Satin's movements intensified, and she latched on thoroughly to Imani. The strap on pushed against Satin's clit making her cum enormously. When she regained her composure she and Imani 69 all night. Of course Satin coached Imani every step of the way being it was her first time with a woman.

Chapter 23

Labor day September 3, 2001

For the next couple of months where you saw Satin, you saw Imani. Satin was showing Imani the ropes. To Imani Satin was the female version of Bob. She constantly drilled quotes in her head to live by.

Most nights Satin and Imani broke the bank giving Bob his cut off the top of course. Satin wasn't big on saving. She was all for living in the moment constantly shopping for new digs to wear at the club. Imani was adopting her habits.

"What do you think of these?" Imani held up a pair of black boots.

"The heel isn't high enough youngin'," Satin said screwing up her face in disapproval.

"I always get two inches" Imani puffed placing the display shoe back onto the counter full of boxes.

"That's the problem. The stacks of money you bring in need to be higher the heel the closer you are to God. Give yaself something to aim for," Satin said picking up shoes and checking the price tags. "Besides, you need something red!" Satin reached above her head and pulled down a pair of fire engine red six inch heels. She then asked an employee to find a size seven for Imani.

Satin dropped off Imani back at Bob's house. They had a few hours before they were due at the club.

"Hey baby," a woman sitting next door on her front steps smoking a Newport 100 said.

"Hi Ms. Jean," Imani said to the neighbor and took her bags in the house as Satin peeled off. "Wassup?" Imani greeted Bob.

"How are you?" Bob asked properly.

"Fine!" Imani exclaimed showcasing her shopping bags.

Bob looked inside the bag. He saw a sexy cowgirl g string costume with red high heels. "Satin is really doing a number on you," Bob commented, and Imani paid him no mind.

She pressed the outfit against herself giving herself a visual of how shed look to the crowd of tippers.

*****

Tonight the club had a two-dollar drink and cigar special going on. The line to get in curved around the block. The heavy clouds of cigar smoke made it hard to see, However, through twenty/ twenty vision eyes you can see the countless never ending shakes and flapping of sweaty bare ass and titties from the stage and throughout the crowd.

Satin was gracing the stage wearing nothing but a cubic zirconia piece that covered her vagina only. The ones fell from the air as she gyrated her hips. Imani sat by the bar flirting with nearby young men letting them get their feels on all in the name of a dollar.

"Baby, you don't got to be here doing this I can take care of you," one man said.

"Is that right?" Imani asked wrapping her arms around his neck.

"Baby if I'm lying I'm flying. Do you see any wings?" The man tried to be funny. He then continued by asking "so what is you want? What do you need?"

"I want and need something big" Imani answered sliding her hands seductively from his neck to his inner thigh finally groping his meat. Imani can see the lustful excitement in his eyes. He handed her a hundred-dollar bill. Imani knew what time it was. "I'll meet you later" she whispered in his ear and sealed it with a lick.

Imani began to strut away but felt a tug on her hips. "Damn daddy, I said I be back," she begun to say rudely as she spun around to face the person. She quickly lost the attitude when she recognized the face.

"I don't want no problems beautiful," Ryan said. Imani blushed at the compliment, and Ryan took note of it.

"I'm sorry," Imani finally mustered up to say.

"How they treating you tonight?"

"Good," Imani said patting her garter that held her bills.

"That don't look good enough to me ma," Ryan said blinding Imani with his smile and stud earring. His long hair was in fresh new braids.

Damn boy, Imani thought. "Are you looking for Satin she's on stage" Imani pointed.

Ryan threw his hands in dismissal "I ain't checking for Satin. I'm trying to see what's up with Infinity. Have you heard of her?"

"Yeah I've heard of the skank," Imani joked but at the pit of her stomach was in knots. This fine ass nigga wants me, she questioned herself.

"She's not a skank. She might got a skank profession, but I think she's a winner."

"You don't even know her."

"I would like to get to know her," Ryan openly admitted.

"Get to know her or kiss up, rub up, feel up on it get to know her?" Imani didn't hold back.

Ryan liked her straightforwardness. He pulled her closer to him. They were standing toe to toe and his breath smelled of mints. "Both" he answered.

"When?" Imani asked fighting the urge to kiss his lips off.

"How fast can you get ready?"

Imani held up one finger, and Ryan let go of her. Imani began moving through the crowd to get to the double doors that led to the hallway where the dressing rooms were.

The closer her heels clicked against the floor to the dressing room she heard screaming. Imani began to jog towards the screams. Maybe someone getting raped. Knowing how it felt to be sexually abused, she wouldn't sit by and let the next person go through it. Imani bent down took one heel off and held it in her hand. This would serve as a good weapon she thought.

Imani pushed the dressing room open with her left hand and stopped dead in her tracks. It wasn't a rape at all. Bob was standing on top of Whynetta repeatedly whipping her back with a belt. Her skin was cracking, and welps were forming. Whynetta was trying to squirm away, but Bob would just drag her back to his line of vision by the leg. It really looked like a modern day slave beating from the master.

"Bob!" Imani screamed.

Bob was broken out of his abusive trance and focused his eyes to Imani. Imani stood there with one heel on, one heel off fear and confusion stamped on her face. "Bitch don't you ever keep my money from me!" Bob said spitting on Whynetta who laid there shaking in pain. Bob walked over to Imani putting his belt back on. Imani had never seen this side of Bob. "Are you okay?" Changing his stern tone to one of concern.

"Yes."

"Are you sure?" Bob tried to caress Imani's chin, but she moved away with an attitude. She folded her arms. How cute he thought. "Well, what can I help you with?"

"I have a trick."

"Who?"

"Ryan."

Bob scratched his chin, "oh okay. Just remember C.O.D."

"Cash on delivery I know," Imani said taking that as her Que to exit once she grabbed jeans and a t-shirt out of her locker.

Chapter 24

Early morning September 4, 2001

Imani scanned the crowded club frantically for Ryan. When they laid eyes on each other Ryan stood at the entrance. He mouthed the phrase come on, and Imani did so eagerly.

Ryan held the door open for Imani, "Ladies first" and he watched her ass as she walked out of the door in front of him.

The walk to the Buick was a silent one. They didn't know each other outside of the club, and it seemed the flirting had gone out the window.

Once at the car, Imani noticed the k was missing from the Buick logo on the back of the car. *Damn he's not the come up,* Imani thought to herself. Satin had drilled it into her head to land a trick with real money

Ryan opened the passenger door for her, and she got in. He closed the door and walked to the driver's side. Once the key was placed in the ignition, Imani broke the silence.

"Sup with you and Satin anyway?"

Ryan cut his eye "why you worried about the next bitch?"

"I'm not but-"

"Clearly, you are" Ryan interjected." Don't be 'cause she wouldn't be worried about you.”

Ryan had cut her off with those words, and she refused to believe it as true. Satin had been good to her. Sure they had their one night, but it was all in the name of the game. Ryan could tell Imani was thinking too much.

"Look I'm just her supplier. You know how Satin like to get big high. She spend good money with me. Sometimes I do with her too. A lap dance here or there. But she doesn't do nothing for me to be fucking her or fucking with her," Ryan explained.

"So what do I do for you?"

"You ask a lot of questions shorty."

"I thought you wanted to get to know me?" Imani asked.

"Yes, you my nigga. I ain't say shit about you getting to know me my nigga" Ryan said, and they both fell into laughter. They pulled up to a dark street with not many homes. Two of the houses were abandoned. The cardboard boxes covered the front doors and windows.

Imani followed Ryan nervously holding her elbows.

"We have to go around back," Ryan told Imani over his shoulder. Once they reached the back door, Ryan unlocked the door with his keys. The house was completely empty - no furniture what so ever.

Ryan gently grabbed Imani's hand and lead the way. He first stopped at a door in the hallway that was closed with a large amount of paint chipping off. He opened the door, and Imani knew it was a basement. The closer they got to the bottom of the basement they seen a light was on.

"Good evening ladies" Ryan spoke to the basement full of girls. It was a mixed age group, and all of the girls were topless. They wore doctors mask while cutting up the dope on a big table. A small table had the baggies on it which they would later be in. An even smaller table had vials of crack in it and dime bags of weed. In the back of the basement were stoves.

He brought me to a damn dope house! Imani thought.

"Hi Ryan, " the females said in unison.

"Now why isn't anybody in the living room listening out for the door?" Ryan asked.

"Cause it ain't no seats up there" one female answered.

Ryan sucked his teeth, "whatever I'll get y'all bitches a recliner tomorrow." With that, Ryan turned back up the steps, and Imani went to follow. She could feel eyes on her. One of the females gave Imani a hard mug and Imani served the look right back.

Ryan let Imani to the top floor, to the master bedroom. The bedroom was completely furnished and laced in the newest fixtures, TV, and video games. Carpet lined most of the floor with some polished tiles peeking out of the edges. The scent fumed of old weed smoke. The queen size bed was covered in black cotton sheets.

"This is where you bring all ya females?"

"Maybe," Ryan smiled laying back on the bed.

"You live here?"

"Not at all baby girl. That wouldn't be smart to lay my head where I do my dirt. I kick it here from time to time, though." Ryan said taking off his shoes. He took his gun out of his boxers and placed it on a nearby dresser. In the dresser, he removed a Trojan condom and a bag of weed with a pack of Dutch Masters from the draw. "Turn the TV on sweetie" Ryan instructed.

Imani did as she was told. Once the television was on it was already playing comic view. She kept it there.

"Oh this my shit!" Ryan said rolling the blunt.

"Oh yeah, " Imani said getting comfortable and sitting closer to Ryan. They sat with Ryan's hand around Imani laughing loudly to the comics, passing the blunt back and forth.

As the night went on Imani learned that Ryan was eighteen years old. He prided himself on looking good other than that he hated being flashy. He didn't want any added attention. Henceforth why his dope house and the car appeared to be so raggedy. It was all in the name of the game. The projects knew he was a respectable hustler whom sometimes had a murderous edge, but nobody ever thought he was full of money. To the contrary, his money was long. His mindset was get money or die trying. Plus, save, save, save money for a rainy day. When his mom found herself a homeless single parent Ryan told himself never be unprepared, for just in case moments.

At the age of thirteen, he was in and out of detention centers for trying to steal from local stores or extort dealers. When the street side of Ryan rested, he was a loveable kid.

Always down for a good time and laugh. That was the side Imani was experiencing right now.

"So is infinity your real name?"

"Of course not," she gave him a dumbfounded look.

"Well, can I know it?"

"Nope," Imani smiled.

"So how did you end up at the club?" Ryan sat up stroking the top of her hair.

"Long story," Imani huffed shifting uncomfortably.

Ryan placed his hands up in surrender, "Okay okay! So what is your game plan now that you are there?"

"I don't know. Eventually move out and get my own spot."

"That plan seems shaky baby girl," Ryan said immediately making Imani offended.

She felt like a dumb lost little girl all over again. "Look a lot of things in this world is shaky aight. So I don't wanna hear that shit! I ain't trying to get caught up with none of these niggas. I don't plan on having no kids. I just want bread to survive. I'm gonna get it by hook or crook," Imani explained defensively.

Ryan blew an O to a new blunt, "Okay okay but are you saving?"

"Kinda hard to save when ya money going right back towards gear for the club or transportation."

Ryan could see the conflict within herself through Imani's eyes like she ain't have a clue to what she was doing. Ryan put out the blunt and kissed her gently on the chin. He made his way to her mouth, and she took in his tongue graciously.

Ryan saw the pain of the past in Imani's eyes and still saw a glimmer of innocence still in her. She wasn't completely corrupted yet. The way Ryan kissed her made her feel safe. Just as she was getting comfortable and extremely turned on by him, she paused.

" I need my money."

Ryan dug in his jeans and placed six hundred dollars in her hand. She stuffed it in her jeans. It was well over the going rate. Ryan mounted on top of Imani showering her with kisses never taking off his clothes. He stepped one leg out of his jeans. When he pulled his erect member out of his opening of his boxers, Imani went to work.

His throbbing manhood leaked precum in her mouth, and he threw his head back in enjoyment. The condom was right beside them, but he never reached for it. Ryan beat the pussy up raw pulling out just in time to let his kids off on her stomach. He took a nearby blanket and wiped Imani off. Imani got on the floor trying to redress.

"Ayo, what you doing?" Ryan questioned.

"Getting dressed!"

" Stay ya ass naked! That money I gave you solidifies that pussy is mine. Why else would I hit it unprotected."

"Okay daddy," Imani giggled. She was flattered he wanted her. Imani felt bad though that they met under these circumstances. In another lifetime it could've been a real relationship. He seemed cool.

Ryan stood completely nude now and completely happy with his decision in bringing Imani over. "Now bounce that shit for daddy!"

****✝*

Imani arose from her slumber around 4 p.m., she had completely forgotten Ryan and her had been fucking like rabbits all night. Imani leaped up quickly tossing the covers aside exposing her nudity. She saw traces of her clothes scattered across the bedroom Imani glanced over and saw Ryan completely nude peacefully asleep with a smile on his face. even on the soft his penis was bold and beautiful.

Imani smiled and draped her body on top of his. For a second she wanted to pretend this was a real love and not an even exchange.

"Baby, what time is it?" A tart breath Ryan asked. Imani moved off of him and looked at the clock on the television.

"It's 4:05 boo," Ryan flung up rapidly.

"Get dressed I'mma take you home. I got moves to make."

Ryan and Imani fully dressed in the same clothes from yesterday crept out the back door and walked around the corner back to his Buick.

"Shit!" Ryan exclaimed. he looked down at his flat tire. It looked as if someone slashed it.

"Damn which one of ya hoes did you piss off?" Imani tried to joke to lighten the mood. If looks could kill Imani would have been outlined in white chalk by the stare from Ryan. He didn't find anything amusing.

Ryan led her by the hand through several blocks getting on the main street. He pointed his index finger and began to flag down a hack (random ride from a stranger to provide cab services). A grey Lincoln finally slowed up. Ryan approached the car first. "Sir, can you take this young lady home?"

"Sure the driver answered. Ryan tossed the driver a hundred-dollar bill. He opened the door to the backseat and awaited for Imani to get in. Ryan grabbed her by the hand pulling it close to his chest.

"Sorry, I couldn't take you myself. I'll stop by the club tonight."

"Okay," Imani said softly.

Their attention turned to a group of people loudly chattering over a dice game. Ryan's eyes fixed on it as if he was eyeing a delicious meal on a plate. The nice Ryan had taken a backseat to the mischievous Ryan pulling a few bills out of his pocket he gave it to Imani.

"Save the money I gave you last night. You can do whatever with this," he closed the door and walked in the direction of the dice game. As the car drove away, Imani never looked off of Ryan. She witnessed Ryan smacking a girl over the head with the butt of his gun. As soon as the remaining group tried to run Ryan blasted off hitting a young man in the throat. Imani couldn't tell what else was happening as the car got out of a reasonable distance.

*****

When pulling up to Bob's house, Imani's thoughts were still consumed of Ryan. He was cool, and she had a decent time with him. Damn I hope he ain't hurt or caught up, Imani thought. Trick or no trick she hoped he came out okay with the mess he started at the dice game. Bob was already outside on the steps talking to the neighbor Ms. Jean when Imani stepped out the car. Once Bob's eyes realized it was Imani, he ended the conversation with Ms. Jean abruptly. Imani never got a chance to speak before Bob was pulling on her arm dragging her to his vehicle.

"We gotta go!" Bob said.

Imani sat in the passenger side with folded arms. "Where we going? I haven't washed my ass or brushed my teeth!"

"Cut the attitude! You took a hundred dollars from a trick last night and didn't fuck him all cause you too busy with Ryan. Your gonna meet dude right now so he don't go upside ya head," Bob scolded.

Imani couldn't protest. She did take the money, and she did have every intent on letting him get his money's worth but got side tracked with Ryan.

They pulled up to a street off of liberty rd. Bob rang the doorbell and seconds later the door flung open. They guy from last night appeared.

"Rock she's all yours," Bob said, and Imani stepped inside the house. Bob walked back to his car, and rock closed the door

"I'm sorry about last night," Imani said eyes glued to the floor. She was actually scared. He was much bigger than he appeared to be last night. 6'8,"270 pounds with bold, broad shoulders and a gapped tooth smile.

The house was filled with furniture from the 1970's.

"Don't be sorry hoe just strip!" Rock demanded sitting on the couch. Imani did, but she did it slowly in attempts to be sexy. Not making eye contact with Rock she noticed boxing trophies, medals, and momentum around

He must be a boxer. I'm definitely not getting on his bad side. After witnessing Bob black out, she never wanted to experience that like Whynetta did. When Imani finally looked Rock's way he sat on the couch with his dick in hand masturbating. The sight of Imani's perky boobs, wide hips, and bald coochie drove him nuts.

Imani walked over rubbing her privates against his as if she was at the club still giving lap dances. Rock moaned. His penis was the smallest thing on his body. It was short in length and didn't have much width.

Nonetheless, Imani kissed rock all over while playing with herself. He rolled the condom not wanting to wait another moment to feel her insides. immediately Imani got on all fours arching her back to receive back shots.

His big ass ain't crushing me, she thought, refusing to do missionary. "Get this pussy," Imani screamed as he entered. Her muscles flexed as she braced herself on the arm of the couch.

"Oh shit!" Moaned Rock repeatedly with each stroke making slapping sounds when his balls hit her big ass. The rain from his face drenched Imani's back. he went for broke on her trying to serve her pain for standing him up the night before. All the noises Imani made you would assume he was killing the pussy, but Imani was faking it.

*****

Rock kept Imani till about 8 pm. After his first nut, he slept and snored like a bear. He demanded a round two when he awoke. When they were finished, Imani asked to go to the closest store to pick up a change of clothes.

"Sure sweet pussy," was Rock's answer.

Rock drove Imani to a shopping center in Walbrook Junction. Imani went into the first store and grabbed mouthwash, underwear, a tank top and some tights. Imani got back in the car after making her purchase. "Can you drop me off at the club now?" Imani asked. Ryan peeled off headed to the club.

When they arrived the parking lot seemed fairly empty. "I appreciate you, daddy," Imani gave her fakest smile. She put her hand on the door handle to exit the car and Rock grabbed her.

"What's the rush. The club ain't jumping yet" Rock said. He pulled out his small, semi fat penis and put it in her mouth. Rock leaned his head against the headrest while Imani took him to another world.

Chapter 25

September 5, 2001

Imani spit Rock's semen onto the concrete when she got out the car. She proceeded to walk to the entrance of the club and squinted her eyes at the figure awaiting by the door.

"Ryan I am sorry I had to," Imani said feeling a tug at her heart to explain herself.

"Chalk it up to the game," Ryan said, trying to wipe the disappointment off of his face.

"So what's up? It's a little early."

"I know. I was in the area after I got my new tire. besides I had something to give you."

"What? You've done enough" Imani raised an eyebrow.

Ryan chuckled, "Hold ya hand out!"

Imani curved her lip to the side but did what she was told. He placed a Diamond ankle bracelet in her hands. "It's beautiful," Imani said admiring it. "I can't accept this."

Ryan sucked his teeth, "Better go ahead with that modest bullshit!" Imani just laughed. "Look here's my number. I'll check you later " Ryan handed Imani a crumbled piece of paper with his pager number on it. Imani didn't have a pager yet. With that, Ryan strolled away and Imani entered the club.

Imani made her way to the dressing room. "Wassup," she casually spoke to Whynetta. Whynetta nodded. She was bruised up, but she was still down to make a dollar. Imani washed up in the sink. It felt good to be out of yesterday's clothes. She went to her locker to pull out a customer. Imani quickly dressed and oiled herself. The heels she wore wouldn't allow herself to comfortably wear the ankle bracelet Ryan brought. "Save it for another time Ryan" she caught herself saying out loud. Imani tucked it in her make-up kit thinking it was away safely she placed it in her locker peeled off three hundred eighty dollars (sixty for Rock, three hundred and twenty for Ryan) to give it to Bob and headed to the main stage.

    ****

It was a slow night. Imani managed to walk away with two hundred dollars after giving Bob his cut. She rushed to her locker to change into the tank top and stockings she brought earlier. Imani got dressed and thought about going to Bob's office to call Ryan. The thought of Ryan made her think about the ankle bracelet.

She dug in her make-up kit, and the bracelet was gone. What the fuck she thought as she spilled the entire make-up kit on floor frantically looking for the bracelet. She found nothing.

"Which one of y'all bitches got my shit?!" Imani asked with her chest heaving up and down. Some dancers looked in Imani's direction, but nobody answered.

Imani could feel her blood boiling. Her hands were itching to make a fist, and her jaw was tight. She was a girl who wasn't used to having much wasn't gonna take this lying down. Imani wanted to enjoy and accumulate nice things in life just like the next. These bitches were in the way of that.

Imani walked over to Shyne and Keke who were sitting together putting on their tennis shoes to make their exit. "Y'all bitches got my shit?" Imani questioned, and the two dancers didn't know if she was asking or accusing.

Keke- chocolate complexion, full lips, and crescent shaped eyes spoke first. "Boo you ain't never have shit to steal. So please don't look my way."

"Why the fuck would you ask us first anyway?" Shyne asked defensively.

"Cause bitch Satin told me y'all some thieving ass hoes" Imani blurted out in anger. No sooner than the words left her mouth, she regretted it. She didn't plan to dry snitch.

"Oh yeah?!" Shyne stood up and brushed past Imani causing them to tap shoulders.

Satin was in the corner watching the whole scene play but as Shyne approached her she pretended to count her money. "Bitch why you runnin' ya mouth?" Shyne asked plopping one foot on a nearby bench.

"I don't know what you talking about " Satin responded nonchalantly.

"Don't act clueless now hoe! That girl don't know me from a can of paint to say some shit like that. Only bitch she been with is a triflin', manipulative ass."

"So you can throw insults my way but can't nobody talk about you," Satin said throwing her money in her purse.

"Naw Bitch I'm saying it to ya face that's the difference!" Shyne moved closer to Satin. They could smell the cheap liquor on each other's breath. In reality, Satin didn't want problems with Shyne. Shyne and Satin had grown up in the same hood together. There been numerous times Satin seen Shyne fighting for her life and Shyne always coming out on top. She had seen her send someone to the hospital twice. Satin was never a fighter. She got through life scheming watching shit unfold, and it never traced back to her.

"Look at the shit you started youngin!" Satin adverted her attention to Imani. She was desperate to take the heat off herself.

"Man look.," Imani began to justify herself.

"Naw fuck that shit. You know I'm street but not one to cross" Satin said strategically trying to move around Shyne to get near Imani. In doing so, she knocked over her purse which was on the bench that Shyne had placed her foot. The contents of the purse spilled out - money, lipstick, and a bracelet. Satin tried to quickly recover the items, but it was too late Imani had already made eye contact. Imani's eyes turned black as coal when she jumped over Shyne to land a punch on Satin.

"That's my ankle bracelet bitch!" Imani snatched Satin by the hair and dragged her head into the bench. "Bitch! Bitch! Bitch!" Imani said repeatedly, with every punch she threw.

Satin tried to overpower Imani but to no avail. Satin didn't land a single punch on Imani however she managed to scratch her several times. Imani was landing another haymaker when she felt a shadow hover over her. She didn't have time to look cause next thing she knew she was getting dragged by her neck and receiving massive blows to the head.

Imani bit at the person's ankles to break out of their grasp. Once she got up off of the ground, she saw it was chocolate. Imani threw a wild punch that didn't land and Chocolate, in turn, put her in a headlock. Imani was kicked and punched several times. It felt as if there were several hands doing the damage like an octopus.

"That's some bullshit!" Shyne said as she made her way giving people open palm smacks to the face to let Imani go. Chocolate stumbled backwards as an effect of the smack and Keke constrained her. Just then Bob burst in.

"What the hell going on here?" Bob asked, but no one gave him an answer. Imani was picking herself off the floor while Satin, Chocolate, and Whynetta tried catching their breath. Bob took off his belt " don't make me ask again!"

"Them bitches banked Infinity, and her jewelry was stolen," Keke explained.

"Satin took my jewelry," Imani added.

Bob picked up the Diamond ankle bracelet that was noticeably scattered on the floor amongst other things that fell during the scuffle. Bob shook his head, "Y'all good now? It's off ya chest?" Nobody said anything. "Good! Infinity let's go!" Imani tried to gather her stuff quickly. The other dancers did the same.

Imani gave Satin, Whynetta, and Chocolate the this ain't over glare.

"Bitch keep it pushing! Let me know if you still taste my pussy next time ya kiss Ryan!" You could hear the jealousy and anger all in Satin's voice.

During the course of the night when Satin disappeared to do a line Whynetta was in the dressing room spilling the beans about how she saw Imani pack away a fly ass piece of jewelry. Satin took it at the mention of Ryan's name feeling as though it should have been hers. She had been buying from Ryan for a couple of years, and all of her flirting had gone unnoticed. Or so she thought. The truth is Ryan just didn't vibe with her on that level. Whynetta didn't care about Satin stealing jewelry since she didn't have an allegiance to Imani nor Satin. However, she was mad that Imani watched her helplessly get her ass beat by Bob. Chocolate, on the other hand, had a soft spot for Satin and was tired of Imani beating her up unmercifully.

Bob and Imani walked to the car. Tonight it was an odd brisk wind blowing. Imani clutched her arms for warmth.

"Stay away from the club for a while. Consider this ya suspension" Bob said tossing the bracelet back to Imani.

Chapter 26

September 6, 2001

Imani woke up feeling like a ton of bricks covered her body. With her adrenaline at an all-time high last night, she didn't feel the initial effects of being jumped by the three women. Every time she attempted to arise from the bed her body slumped back down. When she and Bob got back to the house, he fixed her a stiff drink with rum. Imani now felt the effects of that as well.

A tear silently ran down her face thinking of Satin and her coming to blows. She had considered her a mentor and mistaken her for a friend. she wished she would've listened when it came out the horse's mouth herself. nobody in the club is friends.

She felt bad for Satin caring for Ryan who seemed not to have an interest in her. Imani knew all too well how that felt. To feel unspecial to someone you feel like you should matter to hurts.

Man fuck that bitch, Imani thought, regaining her tough facade. Ain't like Ryan, her man. Ryan paying for pussy so I'm not his either. He's a trick, and I'm something to do when there is nothing to do.

About an hour later Imani was finally mobile arounds Bob crib. She soaked in a bath full of Epsom salt and threw on a spaghetti strap shirt and jeans. Bob wasn't there and being on suspension from the club she knew she would often be alone.

Money doesn't sleep so why should I, she reasoned with herself and dialed Ryan's number.

*****†*

"Satin did what?" Ryan asked in disbelief while turning the steering wheel to the right.

"She tried to steal the ankle bracelet ya brought me yo!"

"That's crazy."

"I shouldn't have put it in my locker" Imani said softly.

"Yeah, that was a dumbass move! How she know you got it from me anyway?" Ryan asked going through a light on Mulberry street.

"Maybe cause you the only high roller I've been with lately."

"You need to upgrade ya circle then baby girl if that's true," Ryan said nonchalantly as he took a blunt off his ear and placed it on his lips to be lit.

Imani loved and hated how brutally honest Ryan was. Right, wrong, or indifferent he will tell you.

"Anyways she got to screaming on me next time I kiss you, I'll be tasting you."

"And you believe that!" Ryan said frowning his face up.

Imani shrugged," I don't know what to believe. Niggas be for everyone."

"And so do bitches," Ryan said bluntly. He then smiled, "That's the reality but..." He paused and leaned over to the passenger side to plant a small kiss on Imani's lips. She blushed, and he ate it up. Ryan looked her once over and decided to keep straight up on Broadway. "Yo since we discovered my lips don't taste like Satin's overly used pussy we can go shopping. I love gear, and if you gonna be rolling with me, I gotta get you right."

The first stop was on monument street where he brought all of Imani's hair products and tennis shoes. They quickly got back in the car and rode out to Annapolis, MD.

Annapolis, the capital of Maryland twenty-five Miles of Baltimore and thirty Miles from D.C. Founded on the north shore in 1649, Annapolis has placed a huge role in Maryland's demographic. After moving the royal colony to Anne Arundel's town and renaming it, it quickly grew and became the port of entry for American slave trade. Then during the civil war period, camp parole was set up, and the first Filipino emigrated to Annapolis. later creating a diverse community throughout Maryland.

Annapolis has lots of high class end shopping stores and restaurants due to the house of delegates being housed there. Ryan knew he could lace Imani in Coach, Prada, Gucci, etc.

Imani and Ryan zipped through various stores. they would occasionally get sides look, but Ryan didn't give a fuck. He knew they were getting looks because they were young and black. the white people probably assumed they were gonna steal. Ryan just gave them the evil eye and let Imani look at whatever her heart desires.

"Are we good here?" Imani asked noticing the stares. bad enough she was totally out of her element. she had been shopping with Bob in generally white establishments but Bob was white, so he could catch a break bringing in poor little black girl. This was different.

"Baby girl we gonna live and love like fuck rules. we good!!" He said confidently.

Imani laughed, "for you to be sooo smart and profound you're so hood."

Ryan leaned against a rack of clothes " whatever!"

"This is stuff is really high you sure I can get this?" Imani asked pointing to the price tag.

"You're worth it!" Ryan gave his best Kodak smile.

"I wish you stop looking at me like I'm a Diamond and realize I'm the trash can."

Ryan completely stunned and turned off by the comment went numb, and his eyes went cold. "No! I wish You stop down talking yaself. Even diamonds have flaws. You're alive and beautiful. Ya life may not be picture perfect, but it's worth the picture still. I'm trying show you some good shit, but you'll never appreciate it if you don't love yaself first."

"Well, when ya dope fiend mother pimps you out, and ya own dad won't claim you and trying to fuck you what the fuck is love?" Imani spazzed proceeding to Storm out of the store. Ryan quickly grabbed her hips and pulled her near. He held her from behind. He just wanted her to feel peace for a second.

"Breath baby. It's over I got you."

Imani tried to exhale. She hated revealing her hard knock life. Imani also hated the fact she didn't have family to fall on, and Baltimore's concrete jungle was now raising her. Feed or starve and she chose to eat. She was too young and gone through too much to have any skills to speak of besides sex.

"Next time you start talking that low self-esteem crap I'mma get Satin to snuff you again," Ryan joked.

"I've never been snuffed," Imani answered with a smile.

Chapter 27

April 3, 2002

Over the next several months Imani and Ryan fucked like rabbits at the dope house. He paid her handsomely and spent intimate time with her like a friend. He taught her how to cook and sell drugs, roll weed, and play video games. Ryan put her up on style too. She had more bags than she could store at Bob's home. He even bought her a pager. Ryan wanted to set up Imani 'cause he could see she needed guidance.

"Hey baby," Imani said flopping down in the passenger seat.

"Oh, naw baby girl get that ass up!" Ryan demanded. He placed the car in park and stepped out.

"Let me guess I'm driving?"

"And you know it!"

Ryan had been teaching Imani how to drive for a few weeks now. He would pick her up nightly from the club and let Imani do beginner style driving in parking lots.

During the day he'd take her to main streets. Imani wasn't a pro yet, but she could get to point a to point b. Tonight the club was shut down early due to them finding Satin's dead body in the bathroom. Imani had called Ryan and told them they assumed she overdosed, and she wanted to leave before Bob asked her to help dispose of the body. Bob didn't want any police at his establishment in the chance of being on the paper with bad publicity.

Imani got in the driver's seat and peeled off the way Ryan had taught her. "Anywhere you want me to go in particular?" Imani questioned.

"Just drive" Ryan folded his arms behind his head and rested on the headrest. He trusted that his driving instructor role had made Imani a good enough driver for him to relax.

Imani drove for about forty minutes with no particular destination. The time flew with their mindless chatter.

" how don't you like Kobe?" Ryan painfully asked.

"Just don't!" Imani said while turning on her right signal headed back into the city.

"Why am I discussing ball with a woman anyway?" Ryan shook his head.

"Why am I in a car with a nigga who won't give Kobe his dick back" Imani jokingly insulted him.

"Because I beat that pussy up!" Ryan said pounding his chest like an ape twice.

"Boy, you think so."

"I can show you better than I can tell you" the two made eye contact. It was pure unadulterated lust that lingered within their looks. "Pull over!" Demanded Ryan and she did by a fire hydrant on a semi empty street. Imani placed the car in park and climbed into the back seat.

Her denim skirt rose exposing her meaty thighs as she positioned herself to make room for Ryan. Ryan laid on top of her tickling her nose with his. His breath smelled fresh. he pulled his penis through the fly of his jeans and Imani opened her legs wide to embrace him. With no protection, Ryan shoved only the tip in her moist folds.

"You've been strapping up lately right?"

"I only been with you lately" Imani answered honestly. They spent so much time together she didn't have time for other tricks.

Ryan rocked in a circle hitting all the spots in her vaginal canals causing the Buick to rock as well. Imani's neatly French manicure nails dug into Ryan's shoulders as he stroked so tender, so slow.

Imani could actually say she enjoyed him. He knew how to make her feel like this wasn't a cash for ass exchange. Although it was. That truth would sink back in her mind at the most unappealing times.

Imani's blouse was dangling off of her shoulders exposing the top of her black rhinestone embedded bra. She scooted her bottom closer to Ryan pulling his manhood deeper. He wasn't going to be able to contain himself much longer. A car that had been parked behind them flashed their lights causing Ryan to look up and peer out the foggy back window.

An eerie feeling fell over him, and he slid out of Imani's vagina. "We need to leave. C'mon and hurry up!" Ryan barked, getting into the passenger side. Imani hopped in the driver's side, pulling her skirt back down from her stomach.

She started the ignition and drove off Ryan's murderous eyes had appeared again, and he kept looking through the rearview mirror.

Just as suspected the car that flashed their lights on them were following them. They kept two car spaces behind them but Ryan was already alert.

"Boo make this left!" Ryan said never shifting his focus off the rearview mirror. Imani made the left and went straight. After further inspection, Ryan said "Make another left ," Imani did so immediately.

She wanted to question what the hell was going on but decided against it. She trusted Ryan knew what he was doing.

"Make another left and as soon as you can after that make another!" Ryan said eyes still glued to the car in pursuit of them. He finally broke his gaze to retrieve a gun out of the glove department but was suddenly jolted by a truck hitting the Buick head on. The car in pursuit of them rearended them causing severe whiplash to both Imani and Ryan. Ryan lost hold of the gun and wouldn't have time to retrieve it again due to the passenger door flying open.

Two tall, big, and burley Italian men grabbed Ryan out of the car. Occasionally slapping Ryan around for shits and giggles. Another tall, muscular man grabbed Imani out of the car. She tried to squirm away, but she was no match for the big man. They dragged them both to a limo that just pulled up moments beforehand. Imani and Ryan were tossed roughly inside.

"Welcome to the party," a young slim build Italian boy said. His hair was gelled down, and he wore all black. His New York accent was very thick. Ryan had a confused expression on his face. The other burley men made room for themselves in the limo, and the limo peeled off. "Do you not know why you have this invite?" The young Italian asked.

"Fuck you" Ryan spoke.

The Italian chuckled, "No my friend it is you that is fucked! Do you not recognize this young lady?' He asked thumbing towards the young girl sitting next to her. She too had on all black and had an eye patch over her right eye. Since Ryan said nothing, the young Italian boy went ahead and introduced, "That's Mia, ya know the girl you hit in the eye with the butt of your gun at a dice game. You shot and killed her cousin, my brother- Anthony. I'm Fitz by the way."

His tone sent chills down Imani's back. She knew all of the talking would soon Cease and they would be there dead.

"You see Anthony was here visiting from New York Mia and family in Jew town when your ignorant black monkey self took his life away for a few dollars!" Fitz yelled. "Unfortunately for you, his relatives are the Italian Mafia Capo family. We always serve a plate of revenge cold." Ryan sunk his head down in defeat. "Look at me," Fitz said holding Ryan's head up. The other goons held him by the collar of his shirt. "We do the real bodying. Not a sorry lil nigga like you from Bodymore Murderland. I'mma beast on these streets. ya should've never left witnesses ya black bitch!" Fitz punched Ryan in the mouth causing him to spit blood.

A goon waved a gun in Imani's direction, and she squealed.

"Shut up!" Fitz fumed. At that very moment, Ryan was sorry and regretted bringing that type of drama to Imani. "Is there something you want to say to ya bitch here?" Fitz asked Ryan.

"I don't give a fuck what you do with her. She ain't my bitch. I ride solo dolo. " Ryan answered with blood dripping from his teeth. He was bluffing. Ryan had hoped they would take the bait and leave Imani unharmed. But the fish, Fitz didn't bite.

Fitz snapped his fingers, and one of the Italian goons pulled the trigger on P89 on Imani. She jumped causing the bullet to go through her shoulder instead of her face.

Making a rolling stop, they tossed Imani out of the car assuming they hit a pivotal spot leaving her to die. Imani laid on the ground playing dead but listening to the sounds of screeching tires.

When she couldn't tell the car was out of reach she slowly got up grabbing at her shoulder. Her pager was in the purse in Ryan's Buick so she couldn't page Bob to come to her aide. Shit, she cursed.

Imani began walking nervously looking around making sure Fitz wasn't going to return. She cut down on several streets until she got on a street she knew. No street lights were on this street, and nobody was in sight. She figured at this point to take familiar alleyways to get to Bob's house without being seen or civilians. Imani staggered in agonizing pain to the bullet wound that she wasn't paying attention to what she walked into. She tripped and stumbled over what felt like a ball, but once she looked down, she saw Ryan's severed head clean cut from the neck and shoulders. Imani immediately threw up. She threw up so much she began vomiting the lining of her stomach.

She finally gathered enough strength to walk away crying silently to herself. I'm so sorry Ryan.

Two blocks away was a nearby pay phone. Imani picked it up.

"911 what's your emergency?" The dispatcher spoke.

With tears streaming down her face she replied, "There's been a shooting. I've seen two Caucasian men wounded. She quickly walked away leaving the pay phone off the hook so that the call may be traced so they can get the address. Imani knew lying about the race of the victim would get the police there faster.

She walked for Miles, and her hand was covered in blood from her shoulder, and her feet ached and began to blister. Imani knocked on the neighbors Ms. Jean's door.

Ms. Jean, in her mid-forties, was a registered nurse. She and Bob had a good friendship because she used to strip back in the day. Ms. Jean flung the door open wearing a bath robe dangling a Newport 100 from her lip.

"Oh my goodness child!" her face struck with concern. Imani stepped in the house. Ms. Jean took Imani into the bathroom and grabbed some spare medical tools she had lying around. "What happened to you?" Ms. Jean asked inspecting the wound.

"Wrong place, wrong time I guess."

"Mhmm," Ms. Jean began saying unconvencingly. "You sleep with dogs you end up with fleas." Imani let the words marinate. "You're very lucky dear the bullet went in and out. A few stitches maybe a sling and some pain pills you'll be just fine."

Being that Imani no longer had Bob's house key because that too was in the purse in the book Ms. Jean helped her pick the locks. Imani could've stayed, but she was anxious to be in her own bed. Bob came in an hour later and found Imani stretched across her bed with a towel on the sling holding her arm in place.

Worry lines formed on Bob's forehead. "Lady, what have you gotten yaself into this time?"

Imani said nothing. The tears stung the back of her eyes so she finally released them. Bob climbed on the bed and just held her. He gently wrapped his arms around her waist leaving a friendly gap between them. Bob planted a kiss on her forehead. Imani let the tears flow feeling happy that she was comforted by Bob.

Chapter 28

April 4, 2002

The next day Bob drove Imani to the outskirts of Maryland to a gun range.

"I want you to be able to handle yaself all the way around" is all Bob said to Imani while in the car. When they reached their destination, Bob advised Imani to leave the sling in the car.

"Good day to you, sir," Bob spoke to the gun range employee.

"Hey, Bob good to see you," the two gentlemen shook hands. The employee's eyes gazed upon Imani. "Who is this?"

"A niece " Bob answered nonchalantly.

"Hmph. Right. Well, you know she too young to be in here" the employee said flatly.

"C'mon Bill, you can't grant me this favor?"

"I've done you enough favors," Bill spat.

"So have I for you, my friend," Bob said tapping the glass looking at the gun selection.

Bill raised his hand in surrender "You know I can't tell you no!"

Bob smiled while Bill got them lock and loaded and ready to go. Once on the range, Imani placed her ear buds in and goggles on.

"Are you excited?" Bob asked.

"Kind of," Imani said.

"Lady once your adrenaline pumps from shooting something you'll be excited to come back."

I hope not Imani thought. I'll do it if it's between me or them. But I ain't no mass shooter.

She couldn't bring herself to think that she couldn't kill. She killed her mother.

Bob helped her raise her hands being that her shoulder was hurt and stiff. "Okay Infinity just aim and shoot."

*****

Bob could tell the gun range didn't lift her spirits, but she did learn to be a great shot.

"Where are we at now?" Imani asked with her head pressed against the window.

"BWI," Bob answered. Bob parked and held Imani's hand while they navigated through the busy airport.

When they reached the customer service desk, Bob greeted the elderly employee. "I need two roundtrip tickets to Vegas for me and my niece, please." After small talk with the employee about how great it is to vacation with kids and grandkids. Bob paid and walked away with tickets in hand.

"What the hell is this about?" Imani raised an eyebrow.

"You need to get away. It's like you find yaself in the damndest situations. I have to teach you to make better decisions," Bob explained.

"I'm just dealing with the cards I'm dealt," Imani justified.

"How about we shuffle those cards and create a royal flush."

"Sounds good."

"In Vegas, we can shop and eat and check out shows. We can network and have clientele out there for you and you can go to an etiquette class."

"I like the shopping part since we have no clothes with us" Imani smiled following Bob to gate c.

Chapter 29

April 5,2002

"Really? The first thing you send me on is a boring ass etiquette class. C'mon its Vegas! I ain't never been out of Maryland. Hell, I've never been on a plane," Imani was very excitable. She wanted to explore Vegas, and an etiquette class wasn't on her agenda. She wanted to do any and everything to keep her mind from fluttering to Ryan's severed head rolling down the street. Imani wasn't in love with him, but she wouldn't wish that upon anybody.

"It'll be plenty of time for other stuff!" Bob assured her as the cab made a right hand turn onto the intersection.

"You're not hearing me. I don't want to do it. I don't even need forreal yo."

Bob cut his eye at her "Look at how you just said that. It would be nice for you to be able to say yes mam, no sir. Not curses and Ebonics."

"And your posture," Bob added. "You look upset all the time and unsure of yaself. You always fidget or slouch down."

Imani examined herself. She indeed was slouched down in the back of the cabs leather interior seats.

Bob picked back up, "How will you get out of the hood if your mindset isn't? How will you be a star if you don't know you are?"

Imani began to fidgeting not knowing how to respond to his line of questioning. Bob was doing the same thing Ryan tried to do. They were making her feel things about herself that she didn't see nor feel about herself that she didn't see nor feel about herself. Even though she was gorgeous to others, she didn't feel she was the smartest. She just wanted to live for today. Bob was forcing her to change so she could be a better her tomorrow.

She smiled thinking how sweet Bob and Ryan had been. Although her eyes stung as tears formed, she casted them aside. He lived that life he chose his fate, she thought.

The cab pulled up to a gated community. It was a three story mansion in the same space as a business park. There were more acres and parking spaces beyond what the eyes could see. The cab driver buzzed the bell since his car couldn't go past the locked gate.

"May I help you?" An angelic voice asked through the speaker.

"Yes, I am here for tea time with Mae Rose."

Bob called scooting closer to the cab driver's seat yelling over him.

"Very well sir," the angelic voice answered, and the gate retracted creating an opening for the cab to push through to provide curb side service.

The Vegas sun beamed on Imani's forehead as her and Bob stepped out of the cab. Imani fanned herself secretly wishing she could wear less clothing. Bob had asked her to wear khakis to cover her frame to be appropriate for Mae Rose. Apparently, she would be critiquing everything- style, posture, grammar, etc.

The only thing they had time to grab were khaki's and a I love Vegas shirt out of the airport gift shop. "This will have to do," Bob said at the time of purchase.

Imani and Bob walked up a long curvy ramp that led to the front door of the all-white mansion. The double doors slowly opened with a butler at each side dressed in full auites wearing white linen gloves. There cuff links sparkled when the outside sun shined on it.

Damnnnn, Imani thought. She dared not to say it out loud. She didn't want to risk the chance of embarrassing herself or Bob exposing how underprivileged she truly was.

A woman approached them with a knee length black and white dress with a Diamond broche clipped on the right shoulder. The woman was pale white with tight curls of blonde and grey hair with pursed red lips. The wedding ring she sported on her left hand was just as breath taking as the mansion.

"Bob good to see you," the woman said with a smile kissing Bob on both cheeks. "And this must be?"

"Imani" Bob answered.

"Nice to meet you. I am Mae Rose" she extended out her right hand for Imani to shake. Hesitantly Imani met her hand with Mae Rose's and also received a kiss on each cheek.

161

"My husband is busy running the casino of course so I'll be left to play hostess, tour guide, and teacher today" she chuckled. Even her laugh sounded really bougie to Imani. It made her feel even more uncomfortable. "Would you like a tour first?" Mae Rose asked Imani directly.

"Sure" Imani shrugged her shoulders.

"Yes?" Mae Rose asked.

"Yes, what?" Imani asked raising an eyebrow trying her best not to get annoyed with the bougie lady. *I didn't even want to be here,* Imani thought.

"The proper response my dear is yes please and thank you." Mae Rose coached as she led the way down the foyer. Imani rolled her eyes.

The mansion spilled opulence, luxury, and convenience at every turn. It also had a touch of southern roots. It consisted of five bedrooms, and four bathrooms along with a long kitchen, a workshop hall, home office, library, greenhouse, sports yards, pool, wine cellar, arcade, and sauna. *How many dicks did she have to suck to get this?* Imani thought in sheer ignorance.

Mae Rose led the pair back to the entrance of the home. "I would take you both to the business park bur I would rather have my butler come escort you to the kitchen to relax and have anything you like. Meanwhile Imani and I will have tea and get to business." Mae Rose said keeping her hand at her side.

"That'll be swell," Bob said turning in his Baltimore accent for a blue collar one. Imani had seen him change his speech to fit his surroundings, but this took the cake.

"Very well. Ralph!" Mae Rose called while clapping his hands twice. Ralph appeared from a corner from the house soon after. "Please take Mr. Bob here to the kitchen and be a gracious host for me. Thank you." Ralph nodded and held his hand signaling Bob the way to the kitchen.

Imani fiddled with her fingers dreading being alone with Mae Rose. their worlds were so apart similar to the travel distance of Baltimore to Vegas or so she thought.

"Right this way dear," Mae Rose said leading the way.

"Can I see the business park first?" Imani asked trying to stall.

"It's may I, dear," Mae Rose corrected Imani for the second time. " I wouldn't feel right to show you and not show Bob as well. Besides it's a long way past my three garages in this scorching heat. A hundred and four degrees is a scorcher, don't you agree?"

"Yes," Imani simply said in defeat. She would have to just sit and do the etiquette training whether she wanted to or not.

"It's yes ma'am dear," Mae Rose corrected Imani yet again. Mae Rose took Imani to her home office where there was a porcelain white teapot set waiting on a small round cherry oak table. Nearby was an office desk with a brown leather chair. Behind it was a tall book shelf also in cherry oak where the table and tea was a short, brown leather sectional reminiscent of a couch at a therapist office.

"Please do have a seat," Mae Rose said to Imani.

Imani sat on the sectional. Mae Rose immediately noticed Imani's posture and frowned.

"No, no, no dear! Sit up and shoulders back. You look so unhappy and unsure of yourself," Mae Rose grabbed a book of her bookshelf and placed it on top of Imani's head for balance. *Fuck what she know about it,* Imani thought and steamed on the inside.

This class was supposed to help her but it indeed it was tugging at her inner issues. The book fell of Imani's head several times. "I can't do this shit!"

"Now we will not use vulgar language and you can do this. Don't ever doubt yourself!" Mae Rose picked up the porcelain tea cup and sipped quietly and slowly with her pinky finger raised. "Now we wouldn't want to disappoint your uncle now would we?"

Imani raised her eyebrows in shock and confusion. "He's not my uncle" she mumbled under her breath.

"They never are dear," Mae Rose said giving Imani a wink. Imani smiled.

Maybe she isn't stuck up after all.

Mae Rose talked openly about her upbringing mainly to keep Imani's focus on her rather than the task at hand. Before long Imani balanced the book on her head and maintained great posture without realizing. Mae Rose too had a drug addicted parent. She was an army brat and her dad went to Vietnam and didn't come back the same. The loving home she once had become a harsh shack. Mae Rose's mother Anne decided to take her and younger brother to Kentucky. After years of struggling at dead end jobs Anne stayed at the Derby in hopes of landing a successful jock. That is where Mae Rose learned her art of hustle of refinement and landing a rich man.

In a few hours, Imani learned the difference between a salad fork and a dinner fork to when it's appropriate for a woman to speak all the while crossing their legs.

As a parting gift Mae Rose handed Imani a pamphlet that she could always use to refer back to. "I wanted to also give you these." Mae Rose handing her another piece of paper. In the neatly folded paper there were opera tickets.

"Thank you," Imani said as Bob approached them back in the foyer.

Bob scanned the tickets, "These are greatly appreciated."

"Anything for you brother," Mae Rose said giving the same double kiss she approached them with.

Did I just hear what I think I just heard? Imani questioned.

Mae Rose leaned over to Imani kissing both her cheeks "Take care of yourself."

"Will do" Imani responded.

"Mae Rose can one of your drivers take us to our hotel?" Bob asked.

"I wouldn't have it any other way," Mae Rose smiled.

The black limo made its way from one of the garages to the front entrance of the mansion. Bob opened the door for Imani. "Why thank you good sir," Imani told to Bob. She wanted to show him what she had learned from Mae Rose. She was so excited to be in the limo on the way to do something else.

"I see you have obliged me long enough. The opera is tonight, so I guess we have time to do your favorite thing!" Bob said further inspecting the opera tickets.

Imani showcased a wide grin. She knew what she was about to go on a shopping spree.

Chapter 30

April 9, 2002

It had been a blissful week for Imani. Bob kept her so busy that she didn't have time to pine over Ryan's gruesome death. Imani was able to shop till she dropped and do all sorts of activities- rock climbing, laying poolside, and zip lining. At night Bob would go to one of the nearby clubs on the strip and send Imani back clientele. They were very good tippers leaving Imani with four hundred dollars after Bobs cut of course.

One of the clients was a Vegas night club owner who promised to leave a spot open for Imani to dance once she turns eighteen. That was very promising to Imani. The dancers made way more in one night than she ever did in Baltimore.

Vegas was a big a tourist attraction, and you had to have money to blow to be here. The city alone was vastly approaching the leading top three destination spots. In large part due to five Diamond hotels and entertainment. It's where sin, gambling, and matrimony collide.

Imani loved it all. The hotel room Imani and Bob shared had adjoining rooms. Bob walked through the doors from his past of the room walking into the bathroom where Imani was standing in a towel.

"Sorry I couldn't figure out what to wear since I don't know where we going," Imani said turning to face Bob. Bobs face was turning beat red at the sight of Imani in a towel. He had seen Imani bare skin plenty of times in the strip club, but when sharing living space together, he tried his best to stay at a distance.

"Is that your way of asking?"

"Are you gonna tell me?" Imani nudged his arm. Imani finally regained total control of the wounded shoulder and had put her sling to rest.

"Glad to see your doing best, baby girl," Bob said gently touching her shoulder.

"You're avoiding the question, sir," Imani said, removing Bob's hand off of her shoulder.

"It's early so whatever you want to do except shopping we can do, but you'll need a dress for tonight."

"What's tonight?"

"Our last dinner in Vegas," Bob answered.

Imani had convinced Bob to let her go get a tattoo. He had to go with her since she was underage and needed a guardian to sign off for her.

Imani's hair was full of spiral curls so her age definitely showed in her face. They walked into a shop off the Vegas strip. The parlor was very small. It was much larger shops further down the strip but Imani opted to go to the first one they saw being she was so excited. There were only three stations all in maybe six feet of each other. no walls separated them. The place smelled of ink and stale cigarettes. The leather couch filled with magazine. The walls were covered in graffiti and strobe lights complimenting the party vibe of Las Vegas.

"Welcome to Stylz Tats and Piercings. we will be with you in a few" one of the tattoo artist said.

"Okay thanks" Imani answered excitedly flopping on the leather couch. "I don't even know what I want," Imani said flipping through the magazine pages.

Bob did the same browsing through a portfolio of tattoos. "Are you really going to do this?"

"Yes."

"You're not the least bit intimated?"

"Nope."

"I am afraid you're making an impulsive decision just because were in Vegas," Bob said momentarily taking his focus off of the many tattoo magazines.

"That was funny. Being here in Vegas period was due to your impulsive decision."

Bob had to laugh at Imani's comment. she was correct. Even if she wasn't Imani debated with him. It was like Imani was always apprehensive with Bobs leadership. "Well at least get something meaningful," Bob suggested.

Here we go, Imani thought. Bob was reading her facial expression loud and clear. "What's wrong with what I said?"

"Why are you always trying change me as if I'm not good enough. Ya know I'm living with you because my parents thought the only thing of value with me is lying between my legs. And with you it's still the same shit just a different toilet," Imani began to break her mug down no longer showing interest in the magazines. Bob didn't mean to hit a sore spot. He was just trying to help.

"I didn't mean to offend you. I just want to help you as I stated from the first time we met. now is the situation ideal? Hell no. At least you're in control of your body, your destiny. You speak of change I speak of growth."

"Growth?"

"Yes. How can you be more than a stripper or a piece of ass if you can't learn to listen? Can a caterpillar become a beautiful butterfly if it avoids the cocoon?" Bob laid his riddle on Imani.

A pale, thin male dressed in all black with two lip rings and large gauges in both ears causing them to drop heavily approached them. "What might we be getting done today?"

"My niece wants a tattoo" Bob spoke.

"Okay, no problem. As long as we have your parental consent sir. Does she know what she wants and where?" The guy asked.

Bob turned his attention to Imani daring not to speak for her. Imani looked both men in the eye and answered with assurance "a butterfly on my ankle."

"Okay mam right this way," the guy said leading her to his station. Bob sat close by, filling out the parental consent form and smiled. Imani leaned over and kissed his cheek.

"Something meaningful right unc?"

****

The nightfall brought a coolness after a humid, sultry day. The once bright blue sky became a mystic ocean of blackness. The jet black sky was highlighted with shimmering stars and an illuminated moon. It was breath taking to see via roof top.

Bob surprised Imani with a candlelight dinner just for two on the roof of their hotel. One of Mae Rose's butlers came and acted as their personal butler for the evening.

"Why are you doing all of this for me?" Imani asked.

"Are you going to question me at every turn?"

"Wouldn't you if you were in my shoes?" Imani asked honestly flipping the tomatoes out of her salad.

"You still don't believe you are special?" Imani didn't answer. "Imani look at me!" Bob said in a stern voice causing Imani to sit up. "What makes you any less loveable than a girl born with a silver spoon in her mouth? Nothing! You're smart and beautiful. you have just as much potential as the next person despite your past."

"Stop it!" Imani slammed down on the silver wear. "Stop your lies! Stop your pretending I'm not special. Never was never will be. My mama allowed my virginity to be stolen from a sick ass bastard. My dad hell I don't even know if that's my damn daddy as much as my mom fucked off! But that nigga wanted to fuck me too! You and Ryan keep trying instill this love of self shit to me. It ain't working!" The tears began to form. Bob motioned to hold Imani, but she moved away. "Don't!" Imani pleaded. "Don't fake like you fucking care. don't fake like I'm a somebody."

"The truth is never fake. A million things can happen, and the truth will still remain. I am so sorry for what you've been through, but roses still bloom in the concrete." Bob explained grabbing her and locking his embrace.

The butler was coming back with the main course, but Bob shooed him away. "Do you believe me?"

"I guess," Imani said with her head buried in his chest soaking him with her tears.

"I'll take that for now" Bob eased his strong hold on her and went back to his seat.

Imani wiped her smeared mascara off with a dinner napkin. "So how did you get to be so smooth?" Imani asked trying to lighten the mood. She didn't want to be emotional anymore.

"That's for me to know and you to find out," Bob said jokingly.

"You're so old" Imani chuckled gazing into the moon. "its beautiful out here."

"Just like you," Bob said, and Imani decided against protesting his compliment.

She wore a navy blue and gold chiffon tea length evening gown with an A-line. Imani wore gold studs not to take away from her Shirley Temple curls. She looked young yet sophisticated. Bob was pleased with her attire. Her nails polished in gold and her two inch heels accented the entire look.

The butler figured they had regained their composure and reentered with the main course. They were presented with stuffed lobster tail, asparagus, and a baked potato.

"I hope you like lobster," Bob said cutting into his asparagus.

"To be honest, I haven't had a lot of choices growing up so I'm still trying figure out if I'm a seafood lover or an Italian lover," Imani smiled tasting some of the lobster. "It's chewy."

"Why don't you dip it in some butter. It will make it softer."

Imani, this time, took a chunk of lobster with her fork and dipped it in the bowl of butter and ate. She smiled.

"See," Bob said delighted that she had finally listened to him without any back talk.

"Mhmm. Much better now!"

"So what do you like doing besides shopping?" Bob asked her. He had housed her for a while now, but he barely knew her.

"Now that I met you I like traveling. It's good to leave Baltimore for a while. it's like stepping outside yaself."

"Anything else?" Bob asked scoffing down more food.

"I like Looney Toons and the Animaniacs. I used to watch it a lot when I'd wait for my mother to come back home," Imani let out a huge sigh. "I also like video games thanks to Ryann."

Bob paused from devouring the remainder of his plate." I saw you spending a lot of time with Ryan."

"He was a faithful trick I guess" Imani answered nonchalantly.

"What happened to Ryan?" Bob was dying to know ever since he came home and saw her in the sling. He assumed she would be too fragile to talk about it. He was just glad she was alive.

"He's not of this world anymore," Imani said fighting back the tears that formed as the wind suddenly picked up.

The table cloth swayed as Imani's curls flung in her face. A helicopter was getting closer towards them.

"Surprise!" Bob shouted over the loud sounds of the blades of the helicopter.

"What's going on?" Imani asked while holding her dress down so that it wouldn't rise up with the gust of wind.

"It's called dinner in the sky, " Bob said extending his hand to help Imani get aboard.

"Good evening," the pilot said.

"Good evening," Bob and Imani said in unison.

The helicopter took them on a tour of Vegas and the nearby valleys.

"Look!" Imani squealed like a school girl clutching Bobs hands. Bob embraced her hands back never letting go the rest of the ride.

*****

Imani had fell asleep the last leg of the tour. Her excitement wore her down. Bob carried her in his arms, off the helicopter, down the hotel rooftop steps, to their adjoining rooms. He placed her as gently as he could on the bed with his body hovering over hers. Bob tried to subtly ease his body away from hers however he was stopped by Imani clutching her two hands behind his neck. She pulled him back towards her and kissed him.

Bob pulled away not wanting to enjoy the soft, supple kisses. Imani pulled him back closer and again he tugged away. He felt so conflicted.

"You've been through enough. I don't want to complicate things." Bob began to explain.

"But I want to," Imani responded. There was no guilt in her heart.

Holding onto his original answer Bob turned away walking to the door that led to his adjoining room. Imani followed him tugging at his arm.

"Don't let me feel denied again!" She screamed.

Bob halted where he stood. He knew she was referring to her dad that never quite claimed her. Not that he wasn't attracted to Imani it was just that she was too young by birth and mentally to not confuse his kindness for wanting to get in her pants. He knew the helicopter ride had done something to her.

"You don't owe me anything! You don't have to do this" Bob pleaded.

"Once again I want to," Imani said groping him from behind. Her small hands felt good pressing against his rising manhood. There was silence among them, but the intensity was there.

"Fuck! This isn't right at all," Bob finally blurted.

"Someone disagrees," Imani said fondling his erection. Bob put his hands up to his face in frustration and then sighed.

He turned to face Imani. Bob picked Imani up and placed her on the bed. While they kissed his thoughts were screaming she's too young for you, stop it, she's gonna fall for you.

His conscience was ignored once Imani's legs tightened around his waist pressing him inside of her. He shivered upon entry. He had expected to be this good but never had any intentions on finding out.

Imani rolled on top of Bob, kissing his neck while straddling him. She planned to give him her all not because her insides were on fire but because he had climbed over the wall that guarded her heart.

Rhythmically up and down Imani rode causing Bob's toes to curl. Sometimes Bob pumped back like a jack hammer. Imani never reached an orgasm while Bob reached several. This was nothing new to her either. She didn't care she just felt safe in Bob's arms.

For almost a year this man has helped me get money, clothes, and shelter. Never once aiming for my body personally. I appreciate that.

Imani gave herself away to Bob until it was time to head to the airport.

****

April 10, 2002

Once back in town word traveled that Ryan's mom managed to pull together a closed casket funeral. Instead of going to the funeral Imani opted to go to the dope house instead. An opportunity had arisen.

Ryan never left her alone in the dope house. every step she took he was right there. Even if she had to shit or piss.

We were cool, but I guess not that cool, thought Imani. He fucked up though cause over time he showed where his stash was. Being as though Ryan was what flies is to shit Imani couldn't steal anything. She couldn't complain because he kept her laced.

Knock, knock, knock! The sound of the back door made. A young, familiar face opened the door trying to cover her bare breast.

Why would you come to the door like that if you wanted to cover up, Imani thought.

"Ryan's dead you do know that right?" The top less girl said smugly.

"I do, but I left something here, and I want to get it. It would give me closure" Imani forced a tear.

The girl stepped aside letting her in. Imani ran upstairs to that famous bedroom grinning knowing her manipulation worked. In the mattress was a thousand dollars in vials and ten thousand in cash. Ching, Ching!

Imani's eyes grew big. She swiped all the contents in the black gucci purse Ryan had bought her.

Walking back down the stairs the girl asked: "you found everything you needed?"

Truth be told the only thing Imani could've ever left over at the dope house was panties. That shit they could keep.

"Yes, " she calmly replied.

Imani walked to the bus stop shamelessly.

Chapter 31

April 10, 2002

Imani came back to the house with excitement all across her face. The heavy screen doors slammed causing Bob to wake up. He was sleep on the couch still jet legged from the flight.

"Do you ever just stay in the house?" He questioned.

"I can now" Imani replied patting her gucci purse.

"What's in the bag?" Bob inquired.

Imani opened her purse exposing the inside of it. Bob grabbed some vials and cash. "Where did you get this from?"

"Ryan."

"I know you didn't go to that funeral?" Bob asked feeling perplexed.

"You're absolutely right I didn't," Imani said reaching out for the money but Bob pulled away.

In usual fashion, Bob took his cut which meant all the vials and forty-five percent of the money. The greed that mounted Bob's face left Imani stuck on stupid. Instantly she felt like she had made a mistake.

"Explain to me why exactly I'm splitting this with you?"

"Remember our arrangement. Everything is sixty- forty." Bob said unfazed by Imani's attitude.

"Yes but that's on earned profit not stolen shit," Imani could feel her temper flaring and so did Bob, and he wasn't having it.

"First off your little ass shouldn't be stealing. I mean I'm not the moral police or anything, but I told ya ass a while back no stealing. And furthermore, nobody in this house gonna be pushing drugs either. Your ass living under my roof so abide by my rules. Haven't I treated you well thus far?"

"Yes," Imani answered while sucking her teeth and folding her arms.

"Well okay, then and don't think about withholding money from me either because you do know what will happen correct?" Bob gripped Imani by the hips applying as much pressure as he could to send Imani a painful warning. Imani's mind flashed to Whynetta.

I ain't going out like that, Imani thought. She nodded her head yes.

"Very good now come to daddy." Bob pulled her closer planting gentle kisses on the brim of her nose. Imani whipped out his penis through his slacks and dropped to her knees.

The instant sensation of her cool tongue hitting his manhood made him moan. Imani loved the sound of a man's moan. That was the best way she could tell that she was doing her job well.

He gripped the back of Imani's head controlling the tempo. Bob became forceful and rough while ramming her mouth. She gaged several times gasping for air, but Bob kept bouncing her head up and down.

I can't believe this shit! The night before he treated me like a princess. A nigga gets a little pussy and some extra money and get treated like a trick. Wassup with that? I thought I was special. Maybe he's just having a bad day? Maybe I'm tripping?

Imani continued to give her best and roughest oral performance despite her feelings. She felt conflicted. She felt played.

Chapter 32

August 2006

Imani's was bobs prize in the club and in the sheets. Bringing in more revenue than he could have imagined. Although, he cared about Imani as a person he couldn't see beyond the green.

Imani was still young and impressionable and as the years went on it was easier for Bob to dictate. So much so that Imani never moved out of Bob's house and blew most of what she earned on designer clothes. She loved the fast pace lifestyle and felt whole when Bob was by her side.

Imani had been driving her 95' Lexus illegally for some time now. Today she was finally going to go get her learners permit. "You sure ya girl can hook me up?" Imani questioned.

"Have I ever stirred you wrong before?" Bob shot back knocking on the rusted door.

Not so long later the door opened, and an almond complexion female with ruby red hair and dark lips appeared.

"Hey chardonnay" Bob greeted.

"So are you coming in or are you gonna stand out there lookin' dumb." Chardonnay joked.

Bob smiled pushing Imani inside the house. "By the way, this is Imani."

"What's up" chardonnay nodded.

"Sup with you" Imani gave the nod back.

Chardonnay led the way through the cluttered living room. There were clothes, diapers, and children's toys everywhere. Chardonnay was a typical hood rat in her mid-twenties with three kids. Her entire family has survived off of welfare, and she refused to break the tradition. She was happy to ride the wave. When her check came the first of the month she'd blow it on outfits, parties, men, and weed. Her refrigerator was always stocked with food. It almost resembled a corner store in her kitchen thanks to food stamps. Whenever money was low, she'd do hair on the side. However, she was the plug for falsifying documents. Doctors notes, pay stubs, certificate of death- you name it she had it.

"What y'all want today?" Chardonnay asked moving some toys aside to sit on the Kool-Aid stained couch.

"I need a social security card and birth certificate," Imani said sitting Indian style on the living room in the clearest spot she could find.

"Oh, that's it," Chardonnay said as if it was a piece of cake.

"Yeah you see I'm trying go to MVA today and get my permit ."

"Oh okay, no problem but whose car is that out front?"

"That's mine. I've been driving illegally," Imani admitted.

"So why not continue?"

"Cause I'm trying be official and not get hemmed up by the police. Get the car towed and shit."

"Yes, you're trying be official illegally." Chardonnay let out a laugh, and Bob and Imani joined in.

"She has a point there." Bob chimed.

"I have a good reason," Imani said

"Well tell me all about it this way," Chardonnay said standing up walking to the dining room where she kept her computer, printer, label maker, and fax machine. this part of the house wasn't cluttered. "So what's the good reason?" Asked chardonnay turning on the printer.

"My mom's dead and the man I think is my dad doesn't want nothing to do with me. I've been living under the radar since eight. I never went to the courts to be placed with a temporary guardian. too afraid if I tried they'd put me in foster care. I just need these documents so I can do me," Imani explained.

Imani was now nineteen years old. She was slim thick-skinny yet curvy. Her perky boobs grew, and her hips had spread more over the years. It was a sight to see with her wash board abs stomach and fat booty. Imani exuded more confidence than she possessed as a youngin. Although at times she still felt like that lost little girl yet more often than not she never expressed it. She learned to be a savage. Show no love, love will get you killed.

"I got you girly" chardonnay said beginning to type.

"Mama, mama" a small child's voice entered the room.

"What?" Chardonnay asked in an annoyed tone.

"Deshawn won't give me back my batman toy," the small child answered.

"Uh-uh. Ma he lying" another small child said presuming to be Deshawn.

"Why don't I believe you. your lil ass always bullying ya brother. You need to the cut shit!" Chardonnay scolded.

"Here!" Deshawn said giving the batman check to the other child begrudgingly.

At a glance, the two children could pass for twins. They had the same face and build. Deshawn was just taller.

"Go about ya business! If I hear any more fussing, I'm whopping ass." Chardonnay said over her shoulder eyes glued to the computer screen. The children ran back the way they had come.

"How old are they?" Imani asked.

"Girl they are three and five. Please don't ever have kids!"

"Trust me I won't," Imani shivered at the thought of having kids.

An hour later Chardonnay had finished all the document Imani needed.

"That'll be two hundred and fifty dollars," chardonnay said with her palm out. Imani looked at Bob and Bob turned away. He been on some straight bitch shit lately. Imani peeled off some bills that was in her DKNY wallet and handed it over to Chardonnay. "pleasure doing business with you. make sure you refer me to some people." Chardonnay said popping her gum.

"I always do," Bob said escorting himself out the door. Bob waited for Imani to unlock the doors for him to sit in the passenger seat. When he did, he was met with straight attitude.

"The fuck was all that about?"!

"What's wrong now?" Bob asked sounding exhausted.

"You didn't even pay for me!" Imani exclaimed

"Look baby girl I hooked you up with her. What more do you want?"

"Well if I'm supposed to be your-" Imani was stopped short of her sentence.

"Your what?"! Bob's toned raised.

"Nothing" Imani humbly said putting the car in drive. As quiet as kept Imani grew attached to the old man since Las Vegas. She often thought he wasn't ready to admit his feelings due to their age gap. Imani knew he at least cared for her wellbeing. Bob also didn't cut off the sex between them which clouded Imani's judgement more.

"Where am I taking you or are you going to the MVA with me?" Imani questioned Bob.

"No, take me home to my truck. I have someone to meet."

Imani rolled her eyes. Bob had been spending less time at home and more time out. The only time Imani would see Bob was at the club when he was ready for his cut or a quick blow job. Imani double parked in front of Bob's row home.

"I'll see you at the club," Bob said closing the car door behind him.

Yeah, whatever, Imani thought as she sped off.

****

The club speakers blazed Bubba spark's miss new booty from the DJ booth. The party was definitely popping. High rollers from everywhere was in attendance tonight.

Imani graced the crowd with her presence using a single and ready to mingle persona. She knew with all the new faces around tonight she had to be as swift and cunning as the other dancers. Over the years as her body grew so did her gift of gab and sex appeal. She wore a. The heads were turning every step she took.

"Hey ma," a familiar voice called out to Imani.

"What's going on Mel?" Imani said leaning in for a hug. Mel embraced her while on lookers took a better peak of Imani's ass.

"Chillin with my girl's people's for tonight?" Mel pointed to a few men nearby.

"Ya girl?" Imani raised an eyebrow.

"Yeah, nigga u heard me correctly" Mel laughed.

"So you wave the rainbow flag now?"

"Always have."

"Man you lying!" Imani exclaimed.

"I mean probably. Ya know I've been coming here since before I was old enough to be in this bitch. Me and you both forreal." Mel spoke as Imani nodded in agreeance. "Being the only girl out of all my brother's, coming and here seeing ass and titties all the damn time I mean what u expect!" Mel laughed.

" true, true" Imani said and at further inspection, she noticed a change in Mel. Mel use to come to the club wearing tight jeans and baby doll tees with jewelry to match the color of her sneakers and shirts. Tonight she wore baggy jeans with a black button up and a tie. Her hair was braided straight back. It made her green eyes more noticeable.

"Welcome to the stage, Duchess!" The DJ announced. Duchess gyrated all over the stage in a mint green two piece to Kelis' "I'm Bossy."

"She would pick that song," Mel said, unimpressed.

"Damn, you been visiting here too long for you to say that shit!" Imani laughed.

"Are you going to introduce me to your friend?" A young man asked Mel.

Mel shook her head but obliged anyway. "Infinity, this is Miles. Miles, meet Infinity."

"Pleasure to meet you. You are beautiful," Miles complimented her.

Imani twirled around so he could get a full view of all of her splendor. "Tell me something I don't know daddy."

"What you don't know is I'm from out of town. I've been very busy with high profile celebs. I could use a friend and some normalcy," Miles tried to lay game on her.

"My friends normally buy me a drink," Imani spat.

"What you drinking on?"

"Remy!" Imani said.

"I've never had that before," Miles confessed.

Imani gave him an amused look. She had already pegged him for a square and that confession just confirmed it. No man gonna tell all his business up front and if your so called around celebs all the time you had to been exposed to Remy before. Remy not even expensive.

" you gonna get the lady a drink or not?" Mel chimed in.

"Fuck it I'll buy all of us a round," Miles said to Mel. He walked over to the bartender and ordered three shots of Remy. Imani and Mel followed him over and stood by him.

" I must warn you since this ya first time. Depending upon how u handle ya liquor the initial gulp makes be a killer" Imani spoke to Miles.

"I can hang!" Miles said trying to sound tough to Imani.

"Whatever fool!" Mel shot him down not wanting him to be something he wasn't.

"What do you normally drink?" Imani asked.

"Champagne" Miles answered as the three shots of Remy appeared. "Hey, here we are!" He picked up two drinks one for Imani and the other for himself. Mel picked up her own shot and disappear into the crowd.

Why the fuck would she leave me alone with this square ass nigga, Imani thought.

Miles pulled out a wad of cash pilling off two hundred dollars and giving it to the bartender. "Keep the change," he said.

Her attraction to Miles suddenly arose. Her eyes were like a lioness hungry for a meal.

"What's that look?" He asked.

"Huh?" Imani was embarrassed to be caught slipping.

"Ain't no huh? You looked at me like you wanted to eat me."

"You would like that wouldn't you?" Imani regained her swagger.

"Maybe" he answered playful.

"Well technically I would suck, and u would eat. Only if the price is right."

"Oh yeah," Miles looked over at Imani and saw that her face was serious.

"Yeah daddy," she answered coolly.

" welcome to the stage our favorite girl...Infinity!" The DJ announced with sheer excitement. Imani downed her shot and dragged Miles to the stage with her as TPain's "I'm in Love with A Stripper" played throughout the club.

Imani sat Miles in a chair in the middle of the main stage. She straddled him by hitting a split on his lap. She fed off of every Lyric to the song. She has a body of a goddess- pop goes her booty. When I see you girl- pop goes her booty again.

Miles enjoyed every square inch of Imani's beautiful body that he got to feel and see firsthand stripping and gyrating on top of him. He would be her prop any day of the week.

Forty seconds left into the song Bob had just arrived to the club. This was unlike Bob. The club been popping and people were still being dropped off at the door by the vanload.

Imani watched from the stage Bob speak to the bouncer and making his way over to have a few words with the bartender with a young girl following close behind him. She wanted to jump off the stage and find out what the hell was going on. Instead, she finished her set and gave the young girl quite a few stares as she followed Bob to the main office.

Miles was escorted off the stage, and Imani gathered all of her ones off the floor and made hurried steps to Bob's office. Imani's heart like to have fell out of her chest when she witnessed the young girl sitting at Bob's desk playing on the computer and Bob stroking her hair.

The young girl was rocking a brown apple bottom shirt with green pants and brown suede high heel boots. Her frame was modelesque just with large boobs. She was fair skin with sandy brown hair and grey eyes.

Light skin bitch, Imani thought.

"Well nice of you to show up" Imani finally spoke.

"Hey dear" Bob gave Imani a big hug. He caressed her backside while walking her closer to his computer where the young girl sat. The young girl never looked up, but Imani secretly hoped the girl saw Bob being frisky with her. "I want you to meet someone. We have a big industry party to go to tomorrow, and I need you to show her the ropes. Infinity meet Essence . Essence meet infinity."

"Hi," Essence spoke first in a happy go lucky tone finally breaking her concentration from the computer.

"Wassup," Imani gave a fake smile.

"You girls talk I'll be back I have to take a leak!" Bob said rushing out.

"So how old are you?" Imani asked

"Seventeen." Essence answered still engrossed in the computer.

Imani was jealous she hadn't been able to chill in the office on the computer especially not on ya first night.

"First time?"

"For an audience yes," Essence said still unable to break away from the internet.

I wonder who the fuck was her audience before. "So what ya doing on this computer?"

"Oh, I'm just on MySpace."

"Myspace?" Imani raised an eyebrow.

"You're not on Myspace? Girl it so easy. Sign in for free using an email type some stuff about yaself. You can choose layouts and music you want to your profile. Add ya friends and put them in the order that you feel that you fuck with them." Essence explained.

"Naw I'm not on there. I play video games and get money. I ain't up on the internet."

"It's the newest trend. And I'm going to use it to get money."

"How?"

"I post all my sexy pictures I can get people to seek me out. ya know networking. Eventually, they will come to the club, or I can come to them. Either way its money" Essence spilled her game plan.

The little fucker is smart. I can learn a thing or two from her, Imani thought hating to admit it. But it was the very strategy she used once she created a Myspace account. That very same formula she would apply to her Instagram page years down the road.

"So how do you know Bob?" Imani flat out asked not wanting to pussy foot around the issue.

"Oh I'm fucking him." Essence stated nonchalantly.

Before Imani could rip Essence a new anus, Bob strolled back in the room. "Let me show you to the dressing room because you're on stage next," Bob said escorting Essence out of the office.

Imani felt tears forming, but it wasn't one of anger it was one of frustration. How could she have thought he was just fucking her. Maybe this is just temporary she thought. Why would it matter it wasn't like they were exclusive?

Imani made her way back to the club to get her fill of horny men. One, in particular, was on the brain. She spotted Miles back at the bar with another shot of Remy.

"So you like my choice of drink?" Imani asked.

"It's aight," Miles said swirling the dark liquor around in the glass making the ice cling.

"So are you doing me tonight or what?" Imani asked getting to the chase.

Miles almost spit out his drink at how bold she was. He never met a woman so straight forward. Traveling with celebs, he meets so many scamming to get their taste of the fame and fortune. Imani, however, was raw and aggressive.

"Are you serious?" He asked.

"Is my ass big?" Shot back Imani.

Miles took a look, and a smile took over his face. "When?"

"When the club let out. And by the way it's gonna be six hundred," she was over charging him like shit. The way she saw it he had it and she needed to take the deceased Ryan's advice and save for a rainy day. The way Bob was set up lately, she just didn't know.

"Six hundred?" Miles asked astonished.

"Yup daddy. So take it or leave it!"

Miles thought about when she pulled him on stage and how aroused he was. If how she rotated her hips during that performance was anything like how she rode dick, he had to sample it.

"Okay, okay" Miles humbly said.

"Welcome to the stage our new sexy lady...Essence!" The DJ roared over the mic. T-pains I'm in love with a stripper blazed through the speakers.

That was Imani's song, but she was annoyed it was Essence dancing it to it.

"Hey for an extra one hundred fifty I'll give you a preview right now in the club," Imani said desperate to keep her mind off essences.

Miles excitedly gave Imani a hundred and fifty dollars. She pulled him off the bar stool and led him to a dark corner in the club. It was some people around in that area, but she didn't care. Imani kissed Miles on the lips exuding pure passion. Miles gripped her ass taking in her soft lips that tasted of Remy. She pulled his dick out of his jeans, and it was a decent size. Imani sat on him having her back turned to him easing his dick in her while pulling her panties to the side. Miles threw his head back in ecstasy. Apart of Miles wanted to stop he never had unprotected sex with someone he just met. The way Imani worked her pussy muscles he was stuck on satisfaction verses doing the right thing.

Imani had planned on pocketing the money from this ordeal.

Chapter 33

August 5, 2006

The next evening Bob dropped Imani and Essence off at the industry party that Miles was hosting. Bob was extremely eager to send his favorite Beau's there thinking it would be a cash cow for the ladies but for him in particular.

The party was being held at a hotel. Upon arrival, the party was in full swing, with plenty of people drinking and down to have a good time. Bob seeing this made him confident in his decision. This was the official spot to be.

"It must be over a hundred people here!" Bob shouted to the girls over the loud music.

Further inspecting the scenery Bob noticed a different type of party going on towards the back. There were celebs, big names, and the who's who from different hoods and areas of profession migrated together. Of course, they were wearing expensive clothing and jewelry and sipping on even more expensive liquor and champagne. Out of all the stunting, Miles was almost over looked. In comparison, Miles wasn't as flashy or handsome as the rappers or NBA players he stood beside. The only thing that made him noticeable he was being obnoxious waving a bottle of Cristal around singing the lyrics to a song extremely loud.

"That's where y'all need to be!" Bob said pointing to where the high profile men and Marcus stood. "I'll pick y'all up later. I have to head back to the club." With that, he kissed Imani and Essence both on the forehead and made his departure.

"Damn bout time that nigga left!" Essence exclaimed.

"You don't like having Bob around?" Imani inquired.

"Not really. That nigga be cramping my style acting like a babysitter." Essence said.

"He just making sure we good."

"I can make sure myself good once I latch onto one of these paid motherfuckers" Essence said scanning the room as if she was looking for someone in particular.

This bitch is so sure of herself. Imani envied how she came in overconfident and sure of herself. She had a ready to take on the world attitude. A way of thinking she just started to develop.

"Come on let's go back here with Miles!" Imani said snaking her way through the crowd.

Miles noticed them right away as they situated themselves towards the back. They looked even more beautiful than the previous night. Essence's grey eyes gleamed with her all white ensemble. It had an opening at the breast area showing just enough cleavage which she accented with glitter lotion. Imani had on a black see through shirt with a leather skirt short enough to reveal the color of her panties. The make-up she wore had her face mesmerizing enhancing her natural beauty.

"It's a privilege to be in your presence again sexy," Miles said to Imani.

"I bet," Imani said nonchalantly.

"How are you?" Miles directed his attention to Essence.

"Fine" Essence answered short.

"What y'all ladies need? Anything y'all need I got y'all!" Miles said waving the almost empty bottle of Cristal around.

"I see. You the man huh?" Imani asked.

"Is a pig pink?"

"Aight that's enough of the riddles, yo," Imani said leaning against the wall.

"I ain't ya, yo. I'm ya, baby," Miles said leaning closer to Imani reeking of alcohol and weed.

"What's the celebration?" Imani tried to create a comfortable distance between her and Miles.

"Oh, my mans just signed a fat new NBA contract. Y'all thought his last two years was amazing check him this season! " Miles bragged as if it was himself with the contract.

Essence eyes got wide. That was the fish she wanted to sink her teeth in. She just needed one night with the young millionaire, and he would be guaranteed to come back to her.

"Aye, Miles we need more bottles man." A young NBA player called out.

"Here I come!" Miles shouted and turned back towards Imani and Essence. "Let me take care of my mans and I'll bring y'all ladies back something to drink." With that, he shot off into the sea of people headed to the bar.

"Girl, who he stuntin' for? Seems to me he a damn assistant or some lacky of some kind. He ain't no baller or publicist or manager." Essence sucked her teeth watching Miles disappear into the crowd.

"I see that now. Yo, I don't believe I fucked that clown ass nigga" Imani answered feeling shame settle into her heart.

"Oh, yea girl you fucked up" Essence didn't hold back.

Damn, I don't like this bitch, Imani thought. "Not really. He bust a nut, and I got a few dollars out the deal. So I came out on top" Imani tried to redeem herself. Essence started swaying her hips to the hip hop beat captivating the attention of the young NBA millionaire she so desperately wanted to meet.

" Hey if that was coming out on top to you than boo you deserved the small fry. Me, on the other hand, I'm looking to score big. And I see my opportunity right there!"

The NBA player signaled for Essence to come over to him. She didn't move. Essence was a real snake charmer. She knew making it easy for him would just make her one of many, nothing memorable. She needed him to remember her and crave her. The NBA player finally made his way to her tired of watching her boobs jiggle to the beat. He rather been feeling on them.

"Hey, shorty. Didn't you see me wave you down." The NBA baller said.

"Are you talking to me?" Essence stopped dancing and placed her hair behind her ear lobe.

"Yup!'

"Can't be my name ain't shorty!" Essence shot. *What the fuck is she doing,* Imani thought. She bout to lose this walking bank and I'mma dive in.

"I'm sorry young lady. What is your name?" The player changed his approach.

Imani tried to act as if she fell and tripped into the NBA player. He caught her by the waist, and they briefly made eye contact. She smiled, and he licked his lips.

"I'm Essence, and that's my friend" Essence held out her hand for a shake trying to break up their brief moment.

The NBA player let go of Imani's waist and shook Essence hand. "Nice to meet you both ladies. Especially you Essence."

"Is that right?"

"Scouts honor" the player tried to act so innocent, and it was okay to Essence because she was playing that role as well.

Imani rolled her eyes seeing she had lost her opportunity.

"What brings you here?" The NBA player asked.

"Girls night out. I never go out. Not really my style," Essence was laying it on thick.

"That's refreshing. Most women nowadays stay in the club."

"Not me!" Essence lied.

"Where do you be then?"

"School. I want to open a battered woman's safe house."

"That's deep!" Miles was impressed. It was written all over his face. That's when Essence knew she had to go in for the kill. Imani had to give it to the girl she had much game.

"Well, my mom was killed by her boyfriend who constantly beat the both of us." Essence grey eyes conveyed sadness, and it tugged at the NBA players heart.

"Here's ya bottle young sir," Miles said handing a bottle of champagne over to the NBA player. "And here you go ladies, fresh glasses," Miles handed Imani and Essence a clean empty champagne glass. The ladies held them up so that the NBA player could pour them a drink. After taking a sip, the NBA player wrapped his arms around Essence.

"Can we go to another corner so that I can get to know you more?"

"I'd like that!" Essence said walking side by side with the millionaire player across the room.

"So," Miles said moving closer to Imani. "Are you spending another night with me?" He asked and then taking a sip of Imani's glass of champagne.

Imani stepped back in disgust putting the champagne glass down on a nearby table. She no longer wanted to fuck with the help. She needed to get on the same accord as Essence. Imani wanted a big fish to screw tonight.

"Do you hear me, baby?"

"Huh?" Imani pretended not to hear.

"I said are we fucking tonight?" He said raising his tone a little louder. Bystanders looked over in their direction. Imani wanted to crawl inside of herself from sheer embarrassment.

This nigga drunk and acting real stupid. its best I remove myself from him before I bust a glass across his head. "Excuse me I have to use the ladies room," she said in the nicest tone she could fake. Miles nodded, and Imani quickly made her exit.

All of the money makers were back where she had just come from. She was getting stares from all the locals. Some in which were very cute but she didn't have them on the agenda tonight. She needed to get back in the winner's circle. *I'll just wait till Miles move*, she thought.

"Is that infinity?!" A drunken, familiar voice said.

"Wassup Mel!," Imani said turning to face her. Mel was accompanied by her brothers. "Hey y'all" she waved to them.

"Wassup sexy" Belly spoke first.

"This party," Imani said.

"Yes, it definitely is" Mack included himself in the conversation.

"Y'all on the prowl for some pussy?" Imani inquired with a smirk.

"Yours or in general?" Mac questioned. The group fell into laughter. A popular song played through the air, and Imani began to rock her body. The group taking turns dancing with her. For the first time tonight Imani was just living. Mel caressed Imani's waist while keeping up with her tempo to the

203

beat. A pretty face appeared through the crowd with hell in her eyes. She yanked Mel with all the strength she could muster.

"What the fuck you doing ma?" Mel asked.

"I ain't bring you here to disrespect me," the pretty girl said.

"Lauren ain't nobody disrespecting you!" Mel argued.

"Then why you all in some bitch face?"

"What bitch?" Mel asked confused. The pretty girl pointed to Imani who was dancing with Belly at this point. "Ayo, are you serious? That's just somebody I know. That shit don't mean nothing. Besides, she likes dick. C'mon ill introduce her to you." Mel said attempting to bring Lauren over to Imani. Lauren pulled away.

"I don't wanna meet the bitch!"

Lauren had put emphasis' on the word bitch that caused Belly and Imani to look over. Imani tensed up preparing for war, but Belly gave her the be cool look. Lauren stormed off into the crowd. Under the dim lights, you could make out the shape of whom she was motioning to. It was Miles. Imani cursed under her breathe hoping Lauren wouldn't direct him over their way.

Mel walked back over to her brother's and Imani. "The fuck is the problem?" Belly asked.

"Man she tripping!" Mel answered.

"You don't know how to control ya bitches yet," Belly laughed.

"Ain't shit funny dog," Mel said with attitude arising. "I have a few choice words for her."

"Please don't let this nigga hype you up sis," Mac pleaded.

Mel sighed because she was hurt and embarrassed. This was her first lesbian relationship she'd been in since coming out the closet. Laurens beauty struck her, and her ambition kept Mel's interest, but Lauren was borderline petty. She always found a reason to argue with Mel. Mel was beginning to resent it and was ready to lay the law down. She scanned the room looking for Lauren and saw her by the bathroom entrance with a pretty lady and Miles. Lauren was playing in the girls' hair grinning from ear to ear. Mel knew what time it was. She was trying make her jealous, and she succeed.

"Now she wanna do that shit?" Mel said out loud to nobody in particular.

"What's wrong now?" Imani asked.

"She gonna leave me over here stuck on stupid and she over here in the corner with her cousin goofy ass basically bout to run around the party and whore herself out. I'm not with the shits!"

"Mel, please don't start" Imani pleaded, but it was too late. Mel took off in the crowd like a bull charging at a red flag. "I think ya better get ya, sister," Imani tapped Belly on the stomach.

"She'll be okay," Belly said eyeing a young lady planning to make her a victim. He pulled out a baggie. After all this time getting high was still his past time. Mack rolled his eyes and went to go get his sister. Imani used the opportunity to head back to the winner's circle.

"Can I get a drink daddy?" Imani asked a young man sporting a number twenty-two Diamond chain around his neck.

"Sure beautiful" he replied as he poured her glass of Champagne. "What's ya name?"

"Imani" she answered she didn't want any attachments to the strip club tonight. She quickly learned from Essence playing innocent will get you a lot further.

"That's a pretty name. What does it mean?" The guy asked.

"Sadly, I don't know" she blushed from embarrassment, and he ate it up.

"Nonetheless pretty name for a pretty lady. How old are you?"

"Old enough," Imani answered sweetly, but she was getting tired of the twenty-one questions. Yet she was chalking it up to the game.

"I hear that shit. Well, I'm Lance. Do you wanna dance lil mama?" Lance asked extended his hand out to escort her to the dance floor. Lance stood at six foot seven inches, medium build, perfect goatee, menacing eyes with a complexion a shade darker than chocolate. He wore all black Mark Jacobs ensemble letting the chain be the flashiest item on him.

Lord knows Imani wanted to respond I have other things I wanna do to you besides dance, but that wouldn't go with her innocent persona she was trying portray. "Sure" she answered and followed him to the dance floor.

They danced to about four songs. She flirted with him through her eyes and gave some bogus story of how she was a struggling college student. All of these men here seemed to have a superman complex and wanted to save the damsel I'm distress. Whatever worked cause all Imani saw was green.

"I have a room here won't you stay with me tonight," Lance asked.

"I don't know" Imani pretended to ponder the idea.

"Please," Lance begged.

"Okay," she answered and felt a tug on her elbow. She turned around and saw it was Miles.

Miles was drunker than what he was then when she left him. He had beads of sweat running down his side burns and traces of white powder on the crease of his nostrils. He looked a mess.

"Hey, homie I see you met my girl," Miles said addressing Lance.

"Ya girl?" Asked Lance.

"Yeah, nigga my girl." The liquor and drugs had Miles beefed up.

"Naw I'm not his girl," Imani said.

"Didn't I just tap that pussy last night. How am I not ya nigga?" Miles asked, slurring his words.

"I don't know what you talking about?" Imani faked innocence.

"Look your fucked up right now won't you sit down," Lance tried to reason with him.

"Ain't nobody ask you shit. I just want my girl. You already married anyway" Miles spat.

Long and behold there was a wedding band on his ring finger that Imani so happened to overlook. She didn't give a fuck, though. She knew athletes cheated the most. So the money was good as hers if he didn't want her to become a little rat.

Imani suddenly became very angry. She wasn't trying let the monkey, Miles stop no show. "Look Lance him and I have a mutual friend. That is, it that's all! I should've known he was gonna try to blow my spot up to cock block in hopes of getting me. All that bullshit he kicking, he gotta go!"

"I know you're not trying front on me bitch!" Miles grabbed Imani by the elbow holding as tightly as possible almost knocking the champagne glass out her hands.

"I think you wanna rethink that Miles or ya ass be without a job come morning," he said sternly and then gave a wink. Miles nodded and let go of Imani in submission.

"Let me refill the ladies drink" Miles suggested, and Imani handed her empty glass to Miles. He disappeared into the crowd.

"Are you okay?" Lance asked Imani.

"I am now. Sorry about the vulgar language that's so unladylike."

"No problem you were just defending ya name. Me personally I can't stand a person that lie on their dick or pussy. If you hit, you hit. If you didn't, you didn't." Lance said rubbing Imani's shoulders up and down. Miles made his way back over with Imani's drink. Lance intercepted it from him. Neither of them ever noticed the white substance fizzling in the cup. "Are you ready to go?" Lance asked

Imani nodded, and Lance made her lead the way out of the party. The further she got she could hear a voice shouting something, but Imani couldn't make out what it was.

"Fuck her good. She likes it in her ass too!" Miles yelled very indignantly.

Lance exhaled hoping Imani didn't hear anything that Miles had blurted out. This motherfucker sure likes to cause a scene. Her pussy must be bomb he doing all that. It caused a smirk to creep across Lance's face.

"What's so funny? I wanna laugh too" Imani said.

"Oh nothing sweetheart," Lance said trying to hold back his laughter. They drunkenly staggered their way to the hotel elevator. Lance pressed the up key. He continued to chuckle under his breath.

In the elevator, Imani and Lance tongue did a dance making it hard to breath. Lance fondled her breast from underneath her shirt pressing his pelvic bone against her. She held her hands up in surrender as he pinned them to the elevator wall. His manhood was in full salute pointing at

Imani when the elevator doors opened to the floor that held their destination.

"Is this right? Should we even be doing this?" Imani asked innocently as Lance planted kisses on her neck pushing her in the direction he needed her to go.

Lance gave her a smug look. "C'mon Imani I promise I'll make you feel right." He handed her the champagne glass that Miles had poured. Imani took it to the head.

"What are you going to do for me?"

"I'mma take care of you, ma. I'mma lace you tonight and whenever we together or whenever you need" Lance said the magic words.

"How much further we got to walk," Imani asked feeling like they had roamed the hall for hours. The hallway was long, but it was the intoxication she felt causing time to move slower.

"Babe we are right here," Lance said dropping the hotel key to the floor accidentally.

Imani dropped down to the floor to retrieve the key. With her left hand, she threw the empty champagne glass and got the key. She gave it to Lance and with the right hand she pulled his dick out through his fly stroking it while sucking the tip in one swift motion. Already she made the fatal mistake of not getting the cash before the ass or head in this case. The liquor had her so far gone she didn't think twice about it.

"Oh fuck ma wait" Lance moaned through clenched teeth. He was trying his hardest to put the key in the door to the room. Lance managed to unlock the door successfully just as his eyes were rolling to the back of his head. She was taking him to a place of euphoria that he never experienced, and he has had plenty of practice with groupies on the road.

Stumbling inside they both fell to the ground. Imani's mouth muscles never dropping her treat for the moment. Up and down Imani's head bobbed and Lance kicked the door partially closed.

Lance gave her a smack on the ass feeling more enticed. Right, when he felt an orgasm coming he pulled her face to his and ripped her panties. She sat on him nice and slow. Her womanhood is nice and juicy more than usual.

Imani winced in pain. She slowed up her pace the deeper Lance penetrated her insides. Lance noticed her motions and brought her closer to him.

"If you can't take it all baby say when" Lance coached.

Lance was so huge - long and thick. Twelve inches more like it. She didn't think it would be a challenge the way she slurped on it. Imani had built a no gag reflex, but her pussy muscles was swollen to capacity. However, Imani took this as a personal challenge.

She positioned herself, breathed heavy and took him all in. Imani got into a groove and rocked her body. His toes began to curl, and he gripped her hips tightly. She rode him like a pro on a bike with no handle bars. He laid back receiving all of her glory. she went to work bouncing up and down her ass jiggled on contact. Imani was showing off not knowing how to act. She felt hot physically and internally. She didn't know how to act. Imani just lived in the moment of being a porn star for Lance.

He felt a nut coming on and yet again wanted to refrain from doing so. He at least had to get his favorite position in. To him, it was all about the doggy style. "Face down ass up!" He demanded.

Imani got on her knees and hunched over. She buried her face in the ground and arched her back. Her ass was a sight to see. He rammed her stroking her wildly.

"Damn nigga you trying kill me?!" She managed to say while her face still smothered into the floor.

"I'm trying make sure you good though you feel me," Lance said landing steady harsh strokes while slapping her ass.

"I feel you, daddy," Imani moaned.

Lance pounded her harder and harder until he was ready to explode. He pulled out just in time allowing the cum to splatter all over her backside. "Wait here," he said.

Imani kept her face into the floor. She could hear feet entering and exiting the room. By the time she thought to look up, she felt a warm rag wiping her off. Lance made his way to her face ramming her mouth trying to get hard again. As he did, she felt someone enter her from behind. It felt familiar. She knew she was drunk, but it was no way she could be hallucinating the feeling. The fire she felt was addicting, but her gut was telling her to snap out of it. She wanted to call a timeout and tell Lance she felt funny, but all she could produce was saliva from the constant stroking Lance was doing to her mouth.

"Dogg, did you get her ass?" A familiar voice asked.

"Naw I ain't aim for that hole. You right this bitch do got some good pussy!" Lance concentrated harder on Imani yet still talking to Miles.

"Oh shit!" Miles said pulling out but cum was already dripping inside of her. He didn't have enough yet. He wanted to feel all over. He wanted to own her. He was addicted to her pussy after just one night. Under normal circumstances, he would've tried to sweet talk her, but he was high as a kite off of snorting some shit with Belly and didn't like how Imani tried to front on him. He rammed all nine inches of his dick in Imani's anus causing her to scream. It sounded muffled cause she was choking on Lance's semen. She tried to squirm away, but Miles held her down. Lance exited the room as another player joined in the fun. Imani getting out of her intoxication tried to claw her way out.

"Bitch!" An unfamiliar voice yelled. That's all she heard before feeling glass across her skull.

Chapter 34

August 6, 2006

Bob had come back for Essence and Imani around three in the morning. He searched all corners of the hotel but found neither of them. He called Essence cellphone first, but it automatically went to voicemail. Bob heart sank in his chest. He was pussy whipped by Essence and sincerely hoped she would turn up soon. He called Imani's cellphone, and a young woman picked up.

"Whom am I speaking with?" Bob asked.

"This is Melanie. Some fucked up shit happened Infinity is at the hospital."

"Which one?"

"University"

"You stay there I'm on the way" Bob sprinted to his car. Upon exiting, he could see yellow tape by the elevators as if it was a part of a crime scene.

****

Bob rushed to the hospital. He asked a few desk clerks for whereabouts of Imani and was provided the answers to get to her after showing identification.

Once he reached the room, he was stopped by two detectives. " Hi, sir. May we ask you a few questions?"

"Can this wait. I really need to check on my niece." Bob said looking over their shoulders trying to peer in the room.

"Till only take a minute. We are trying to help your niece." The first detective pleaded.

"Okay, okay" Bob calmly submitted.

"What's ya name and relationship to the vic?" The second officer asked ready to record her findings.

"My name is Bob, and I'm her uncle."

"Where you aware of her whereabouts last night?"

"Yes"

"Is that a normal routine for her?" The female detective asked.

"She's a teenager. What teenager doesn't want to party."

"Does she know anybody at the party she attended?"

"Possibly" he answered shortly not wanting to give much away until he knew what was going on. "Wait y'all drilling me and I don't know what happened. I just know she is here."

"Well, it seems ya niece has been raped vaginally and anally. The suspect or suspects knocked her unconscious with a hotel lamp. As far as we know the hospital swabbed for semen but ya niece doesn't want any chargers pressed. She's over eighteen so you can't consent for her but can you talk to her so we can move forward with the investigation."

Bobs eyes began to swell with tears. He stormed in the room where Imani laid with a bandage around her head. Mel sat in the chair while a nurse stood in the corner and checked Imani's vitals.

"Don't worry. There is no swelling or fluid around the brain. She will be fine," she wrote her findings on the medical chart and started to walk out. "Buzz me if you need anything!"

"What the hell happened to you? Why is it always you? And where is Essence?" Bob hurled off the questions.

No this motherfucker did not. I'm laid up in the hospital, and he worried about his other bitch. " I got my ass beat and raped as you can see. And I don't know where that girl is," Imani had immediately caught an attitude.

Bob felt real small. "I'm sorry. Who did this?"

Imani looked around to see if she saw the detectives. She saw a pants leg of an officer in the hallway. "I don't know."

"How did you end up here?"

"That would be me" Mel chimed in. "Yeah see the party was still going and my girl Lauren and I finally stopped beefing about to head out. I just so happened to turn my head to the right, and I saw a bloody hotel sheet on the floor in front of the elevator. When I saw feet poking out my girl and I ran over called 911. I just stayed once I realized it was Infinity."

"Thank god for you," Bob said with his heart heavy.

The nurse came back in and went to Imani's bedside. "Is it alright if I speak with you in front of them?" Imani nodded yes. "Okay well ya bloodwork came back, and we found drugs and alcohol in your system."

"What weed?' Imani asked.

"No narcotics. How long have you been using?" The nurse asked.

"I've never done drugs aside from weed before. I was drinking champagne, but that would explain a lot," Imani attempted to sit up in bed.

"Well, that's why it isn't good to drink. First of all, you're underage. Alcohol of any kind can mess up with your ability to make clear decisions. And there are all sorts of date rape drugs out there. Whomever you were with took advantage of a situation clearly." The nurse stated.

"That's why you should talk to us and press charges. We can get them on serving alcohol to a minor and rape and battery. You will have justice." The female detective said.

"Naw I'm good" Imani answered plainly. Bob, Mel, and the nurse stood in shock. Bob assumed she was living by the no snitching policy. Mel couldn't phantom who she was trying protect or save face for, but she applauded her inner strength because if the shoe was on the other foot, Mel would want the pervert sent to jail so he himself could be raped.

"Are you sure? You could get these people off the street. let them get their asses handed to them." Mel said.

Imani thought about it. With all the pain she was in something needed to be done. But for the moment she didn't want to deal with the cops. "I'll let you know okay" Imani directed her comment to the two detectives.

"Millions of women let their attacker go free. They are too afraid to speak. Don't be one of them don't be afraid." The female detective said handing Imani a business card. With that, the two officers left.

"Y'all straight?" Mel asked Bob and Imani.

"I'm good I just need to relax. Thanks for everything shorty go chill with ya girl. What's her name?" Imani asked.

"Lauren."

"Yeah Lauren" Imani smiled. Mel dapped her up feeling that was the safest thing to do being that her body was so fragile. She said goodnight to Bob and exited.

"We gotta stop this," Bob said

"Stop what?"

"This extra shit. No more tricks no more private parties." Bob answered feeling somewhere between guilt and rage. "I keep trying protect you and I keep failing," Bob said.

"We both are a gluten for punishment, but I'm a pretty big girl I can make my own choices," Imani answered trying to get comfortable, but every inch of her body hurt to move. "But your right I won't be doing any extra." For now, at least.

*****

Imani had stayed in the hospital a week. The hospital did lots of scans on her head to make sure it wasn't any long-term effects of the injury she sustained. There was nothing to worry about as far aa the doctors could tell.

Imani was glad to be home at first but a week in she stared getting depressed. Often she would wake up in a cold sweat from having flashbacks of parts that she could remember that wasn't totally erased from memory due to the drugs and head blow.

She watched Bob mope around the house for days. He was still guilt ridden of introducing Imani to this way of life, but he was also heartbroken.

Essence had finally called asking Bob to stop calling her and to lose her number. She had moved on with her life and got exactly what she wanted which was the big fish. The millionaire NBA player she snagged was utterly convinced he found a trophy in her. The pussy must've been fire that night or he was drugged to cause the next day they had a quickie wedding in Vegas. As far as Essence was concerned, she was set for life. A marriage with no prenup. Imani was sure shed be plotting a baby soon. She had to give credit where credit was due the girl had game. It tickled Imani's fancy to see Bob so upset over it. She figured once he bounced back they would be how they were.

"Come watch Judge Mathis with me," Imani pleaded. She had been laying on the couch for a week. She was still sore, and the living room was middle ground for everything- kitchen, bathroom, front door. Bob begrudgingly got off the floor and moved to the couch. He still had the expression of a sad puppy dog. "Oh my gosh get over it!" Imani barked.

"What the hell are you talking about?" Bob asked.

'You act like your in pain. I'm the one should be sad. I'm the one in pain. All the bitches you been around for years and you gonna let one piece of pussy tear you down."

"I know I know," Bob said sighing.

"I know nothing about that night went as planned. I didn't plan to get raped. You didn't plan to lose ya bitch, and we both didn't plan to lose out on money" Imani instantly regretted going against the rules of cash for ass and cash on delivery. She must admit Lance played her. She must admit in the same breath she played herself.

"Yeah, we did miss out on a shitload of money. You can gain that back in time just dancing when you're up to it. In the meantime, ill teach you how to keep up the books. You'll be a little business savvy."

"Sounds good to -" Imani never finished her sentence because all the contents of her breakfast came spilling out of her mouth. It was like a faucet it just kept coming. The sight of it was disgusting. It was lumpy and brown. Bob ran to the kitchen to get paper towels and bleach to clean the mess up. "I'm sorry" Imani cried.

"It's okay," Bob replied.

*****

The random vomiting continued for another week and a half. Imani tried to brush it off thinking it was the effects of the painkillers, but Bob wasn't having that.

"I think you should go back to the doctors." Bob pleaded.

"And I think you should drop the issue" Imani spat.

"Why are you so bull headed?"

"Why are you so pushy? Damn first you want me to talk to the cops now you want me to go to the doctors. For what?" Imani said walking to the kitchen.

"If my memory serves me correctly that was Mel who suggested you talk to the cops. I never persuaded you one way or the other even though it's nothing wrong with getting justice legally or illegally. But let's get back to what's really my current concern. You keep throwing up randomly. It happens whether you eat or not. Every day maybe twice a day. That doesn't freak you out?"

"Wow Bob you are really white," Imani made fun of him.

"I'm serious!" Bob exclaimed.

"Okay, okay! I'll make an appointment," Imani said dipping some strawberries in sugar. She raised her hands to her mouth to take a big bite and immediately began to gag. She threw the fruit down holding her mouth with one hand and holding her stomach with the other. Imani ran to the bathroom just in time.

"Imani you're on your own cleaning it up this time. I'm gone to the club" with that Bob was out the door.

Chapter 35

August 16, 2006

Imani never made the appointment. She was still being stubborn as a mule. All she wanted to do was sleep and if she wasn't sleep she fussed at Bob for being in her shit. Bob devised a plan.

"Hey baby girl," Bob said standing in her doorway.

"What?" Imani answered groggily.

"I'm going shopping. Don't you wanna go?" Bob probed her.

"Naw you know I'm always down to shop," she said flinging the covers of her body.

She quickly dressed in a house of Dereon dress. Bob smiled knowing his plan was working. "Am I driving or you?"

"I'm going to drive so when I'm ready to go we can go," Bob said plainly. Imani walked with him to his truck and got into the passenger seat worry free.

After twenty minutes of driving, she realized Bob weren't going to their normal spots. An uneasy feeling fell upon her. "Where are we going?" Imani asked.

Bob stayed silent until they pulled near the university hospital and he could park. He let out a huge sigh with his head down and finally gained the courage to face Imani.

"Look I'm doing this for your own good. We need to find out why you're so sick and sluggish. I have my suspicion, but I'm no doctor. You can't act like a little girl and run from this," Bob spoke.

Imani folded her arms. "We're here now, so I guess I don't have a choice."

Bob slowly got out the car thankful this wasn't an overblown argument that had to be had. He walked over to the passenger side and helped Imani out the car. Bob walked inside the hospital taking her back to the doctors that took care of her during the initial rape.

"Sir this part of the hospital doesn't do walk in visits. You can take her to the emergency room" the clerk said. Bob was beginning to protest, and it further aggravated Imani. She didn't want to be there in the first place. The nurse that had helped Imani during the rape walked in on the conversation recognizing Imani's face.

"What's the problem here?" The nurse asked.

"These people want some test done following some medications that were prescribed." The clerk said nonchalantly.

"This lady here has been through traumatic experience. I think she just feels comfortable with us and doesn't want to be told to go to another section. I know it's not my call but let me speak to her please," the nurse pleaded, and the clerk waved her hands in surrender. The nurse took them to a vacant patient room. "What's going on?"

"I think she's pregnant," Bob blurted out.

"I think it's the medicine. I told y'all I never did drugs hell I've never took medicine before. Never really been to the doctors. This is all new to me so don't pay my uncle no mind," Imani intervened.

"Okay okay stay here we can get a urine sample and blood work." The nurse said.

"Okay," Imani said scooting on the hospital bed.

"What were ya symptoms again?" The nurse asked.

"Throwing up and tired."

"And moody" Bob chimed in. Imani cut her eye at him. The nurse let out a chuckle.

Five minutes later someone came in to draw Imani's blood. The nurse had left Imani a cup to provide a urine sample. She did once her blood was done being drawn. Imani was able to take a nap by the time the nurse came back.

"We are gonna take you off the medicine" the nurse explained.

"See I told you it was the medicine" Imani bragged to Bob. She was elated.

"Actually, you are pregnant." The nurse said placing the lab results back on the clipboard and pinning it under her arms. It was the biggest shock Imani ever experienced. She was speechless. "I'll give you guys a minute" with that the nurse exited.

Imani felt extremely annoyed at what she had just found out. It just felt like a hassle. At least she found out extraordinarily early. She could only be a few weeks. The rape wasn't that long ago.

"What do you want to do?" Bob asked.

Imani rolled her eyes. This motherfucker. She thought the choice was obvious. "I'm not keeping it! " she thought about her getting raped.

Who know who the father is even though if my memory serves me correctly Lance pulled out. Imani think now. Pulling out is never always one hundred percent.

This situation was less than ideal. Imani knew in her heart of hearts she'd be ill suited. There was no motherly bone in her body. Thanks to Levi and Catherine of course. How could she be a parent if she never had one? There were no internal resources.

"When do you wanna do this?" Bob asked.

"The sooner, the better," Imani replied.

****

"Hurry up out the bathroom. we will be late. Your appointment is at eleven!" Bob banged on the bathroom door.

Imani sat on the toilet waiting for the results of the pregnancy test. Two lines appeared. She was definitely pregnant! She didn't know why she was still in a phase of denial.

She put the test under a broke piece of tile in the bathroom and headed to planned parenthood with Bob.

When they got there, Imani signed herself in. Bob remained quiet and held her hand. "I'll be fine," Imani said she could feel that Bob was more nervous than she. She, in all honesty, couldn't wait to get it done. Imani never pictured herself a mother.

A nurse called her name and motioned for Imani to head to the back. Once in the small cold room, Imani was instructed to strip down and place on a hospital gown.

They gave Imani a sonogram first to check everything was in order. They checked the cervix as well. Imani declined getting a sonogram picture or to hear the baby's heartbeat. She didn't want any proof of this moment.

The doctor gave Imani a D&C and asked her to stay for a while to be monitored. "What choice do I have," was Imani's response.

"Would you like ya uncle?" The doctor asked.

"Naw I'mma just sleep," Imani stated. She sat up staring at the ceiling. She thought of the days of drinking water from a toilet, rocking hand me downs and getting molested by Mr. E. She thought about Ryan, Satin, and Levi. All these painful events and she still hasn't risen to the occasion. Sure I have designer things, and now that Essence is out the picture, Bob cares for me again. But I don't have really nothing on my own. I haven't got the big fish that Essence and Satin spoke of. I barley have any money saved like Ryan suggested. What am I really doing? What could I be doing?

She was taken out of her thoughts due to the agonizing pain that penetrated her stomach. Shooting pain went from her back to her abdomen to her toes. She curled up in a fetal position, but it didn't lessen the pain. It had felt like the worst version of menstrual cramps. Imani began having hot flashes. Her mouth was dry and hands were clammy. The pain in her abdomen got worse and worse by the minute. She felt like the devil had struck her twice - first time the pain of the initial rape and second time now the effects of the D&C. Imani was no longer willing to take this lying down. She was gonna come out on top of this. Imani came up with the perfect idea.

Chapter 36

August 26, 2006

It took Imani another week to heal. Bob waited on her hand and foot. Imani was appreciative that Bob was there. She thought she would eventually be an emotional wreck and have some remorse, but those feelings never came. Her thoughts of vengeance kept her busy.

The two detectives showed up at the house trying to persuade Imani to turn in her rape kit and bring her attacker down. She gave them a bogus story of how she just wanted to heal and move on and helping them would prevent that process. Oddly they respected her wishes. They must've heard that a thousand times.

"Are you going out today?" Imani asked Bob.

"I forgot to tell you I have some business to attend to in Vegas. I'm leaving today."

"Okay cool," Imani said calmly.

"Please do me a favor," Bob began

"What's that?"

"Stay in the house. Its plenty of food here. If you get bored and wanna talk, call me, or Ms. Jean next door," Bob pleaded.

"Okay, Bob."

"No, I'm serious!" Bob pestered.

"I know Bob" Imani sighed and gave him a kiss on the cheek. She began helping him pack.

Later that day Imani drove her 95' Lexus for the first time in weeks. She wanted to go to the library and get on the computer. While Bob was away, she was ready to play dirty.

When she got to the library, she signed up for a library card. She found an empty computer and made herself comfortable. She knew for what she had planned she would be there a while. She created a Myspace account.

After some tedious searching, she found some prospects from the club and be friended them. She also began doing a search on celebrities- rappers, comedians, models, and ball players. Imani stumbled upon Essence page who plastered her millionaire NBA husband all over it. Imani clicked on his page. Mhmmm just what the doctor ordered she thought. Essence's husband top eight friends included Lance. The excitement brew within Imani with each click she took.

After doing some google investigation, Imani learned all urls are linked to an email address, and all email address are linked to a mailing address.

The internet is a glorious tool she thought. It took some probing, but she got the email and home address of a very important unsuspecting pawn in this game of chess she was ready to play.

Imani wrote the information down and then googled how to get a P.O. box. The computer read

That was all she had left to do to put this plan in motion. After extending her computer time with the librarian about five times, she had enough information to sit on and head out.

"Do you have all of your research dear?" The elderly librarian asked.

"Yes ma'am," Imani politely answered. *Next stop, the post office,* Imani thought.

****

Imani had gotten herself a P.O. box and mailed off a letter to Lance's wife.

Hello, my name is Allison, and I met your husband Lance at a party. I'm only eighteen, and I guess I can be easily persuaded. I believed his eyes when he told me he love me, and I believed him when he said he would cherish my virginity. I never knew he was married, and I figured that's why I never seen him again. I don't mean you any harm, but I'm pregnant. I'm scared, and my parents found out and are kicking me out. They are extremely religious. I just need him to be a father to my baby. If not, I'll have no choice but to go to press and let the world know about his love child and tarnish his image and ruin his endorsements.

Sincerely,

Allison

Imani didn't know what to expect out of this interaction. She was hoping for a divorce and maybe a little money for her pain and suffering. If she ruined his life just a little, she would be satisfied. Imani put the pregnancy test in a Ziploc bag. She placed the Ziploc bag and letter in a huge manila envelope and mailed it off.

Bob was back in town at this point so she spent most of her time with him. During the day they were home together and at night, she went to the club with him and help maintain his books. For once Imani felt useful. It was a difference between shaking ass and learning accounts receivable, checks, and balances. Right, then she knew she would be a silent partner or investor in a club one day.

"Bob" she called for him from her bedroom.

"What?" He answered.

"I'm feeling a little cramped you mind if I go get my nails done alone."

Bob let out a huge sigh. Truth was Bob got tired of feeling like he had to babysit Imani as well. "I guess I can trust you to do just that right?"

"Scouts honor," Imani said with a smile.

"Very well. I have some new dancers I need to audition anyway. I'll see you later," Bob said walking out of Imani's room and grabbing his car keys off the mantel.

Imani was ecstatic that her plan worked. Bob was very smothering lately, all in the name of protecting her. But it's been a couple of weeks and Imani hadn't checked the P.O. box. she didn't want Bob to find out she was reaching out to Lances wife. *Never let ya right hand know what ya left is doing,* she thought.

Imani arrived at the post office. She had to go through the same formalities. Imani unlocked her P.O. box, and her eyes got wide. Her lips curved uncontrollably to a smile. It was an even bigger manila envelope than what she had sent. She opened it, and money poured out with a note attached.

Dear Allison

I know without a shout of a doubt my husband has been unfaithful. I've caught him several times and kept the shame hidden from friends and family alike. I hope that one day he grows out of this, but I doubt it highly. We have been together since middle school, and he can't seem to keep his dick away from road hoochies. It hurts, but I would be lying to say that I'm gonna leave. I'm not giving up on my husband or the manner in which of become to live. All of my husband's infidelities I will take to my grave and you will too. Here's is $50,000 dollars for you and the baby to stay away and never mention this again. I'll send $3,000 a month until the baby is eighteen.

Sincerely,

Nikki

Well, I'll be god damn. Imani expected some backlash and some hush money but nothing like this. She didn't think women were so desperate to cling onto a man. But whatever the case she was happy. She reread the letter and counted the money a dozen times in her car. Imani knew she was just set for life. Imani took a page out of Essence book and manipulated her way to the big fish, and she would never tell Bob about it.

Chapter 37

present day

Dave and Imani eventually hired a maid to cook and clean for them while they anticipated death to come.

Mama Ross grew tired of wondering where the both of them were. Dave called and asked for a maid referral to keep up appearances.

"Ma I'm sorry we've been in Punta Cana kinda like a second honeymoon. We are jet leg can you please send a maid today."

"I don't give a fuck if the pope needed y'all don't ever drop off the face of the earth and then call me for a fucking favor." Mama Ross scolded. Dave coughed. "Expect a maid in a few hours."

Dave let out a series of coughing, "Thanks, ma."

"Damn boy why are you coughing so much?"

"Think I got a summer cold" the lie rolled off of Dave's tongue freely and effortlessly. He still played his role of a devoted husband trying to protect Imani and respect their privacy. Dave even told Jodi to keep up appearances and not to lay a finger on K.O. He didn't need the heat because then Mama Ross would definitely know something was up.

Imani lay across the bed watching Dave lie to his first queen, his mother. After all, I've done, he still wants to protect me.

Once Dave hung up, they draped across on the bed together holding hands reliving and shedding tears of Imani's fucked up past.

"So before me you never climaxed?" Dave asked still finding it hard to believe considering all the men she slept with.

"I know it's hard to believe. I've slept around...a lot but no. I think mentally I blocked the pleasure. Most people have sexual encounters by choice. Mines was forced, and then it became a survival mechanism. No man not even my own father saw past my physical than you" Imani replied eyes burning trying to hold back tears. It seems lately that's all she could do. Revealing her shameful past and dealing with aids sent her on an emotional rollercoaster.

Dave hung his head low, "Well you were my woman crush. I couldn't get past ya beauty. I'm just as bad as them."

Imani stroked his chin, "you took the time to get to know me and I lied to you. I earned my choice to love you. I stole yours. You married me, and you chose me over ya family. You aren't a bad person. I am! Because of you, I know what real love is and because of me you know what betrayal is," Imani began to sob frantically into his legion filled chest. This dark cloud will never leave the top of my head. Even in death, I'll be consumed with guilt, regret, and sorrow.

Her heart was heavy and Dave must could feel it because he held Imani close and let out a big sigh and whispered, "I forgive you." He sealed it with a forehead kiss and we fell asleep in each other's arms.

Chapter 38

Dave's final words to me was I forgive you. I wish I could feel happy about that, but I don't. I didn't deserve his forgiveness. To be honest, since we found out that we've been stricken with this deadly disease I was hoping to die before him.

Day by day Imani told Mama Ross the truth of Dave's final days and the truth of her past. It was a ball of emotions that came with her truth. The truth, in turn, was met with a fist to Imani's nose. yet they still had to plan Dave's funeral arrangements.

Today was the day of the funeral, and Imani didn't want to be in attendance. *I could say my goodbyes in prayer*, Imani thought. She didn't want people to see or know the embarrassment of a wife he had. Mama Ross insisted Imani's absence would stir more controversy.

Imani wore a beautiful all black dress from Kurvy Girl Apparel- a local shop in Baltimore. to set it off she had Louboutin heels.

The whole city turned out for her late husband. Dave's college friends had wonderfully nice accurate remarks. The repass was held at a hall, but I didn't attend. I went immediately to her house to bury herself in a greater depression.

The maid Marta was there cleaning as usual. "Do you need anything miss?" She asked, but Imani brushed past her like a zombie.

As soon as she reached her room, she dropped to her knees- sobbing, screaming, and throwing whatever that was close by.

My house will never be the same -never be a home again. All these clothes, jewelry, and money didn't mean shit. I was steady trying to cover up for that insecure poor sexually abused girl I was instead of adapting to the grown woman with a husband. The husband who would've allowed me to start fresh to become different and better. I knew better, and I chose not to do better, and now Dave's life is at an end.

Imani was so deep in her remorseful thoughts she never heard Mama Ross come in. Mama Ross hugged her from behind, "that's enough! I've buried two sons and a husband you don't see me on the floor. pull yaself together. Your days are already numbered, and that's punishment enough. You have aids deal with it! Dave is gone deal with it!" Imani tried to refrain from crying, yet her lips kept quivering. Mama Ross continued, "I came over to bring you a plate from the repass."

"I'm not hungry," Imani managed to answer.

"You will eat!" Mama Ross demanded. She sent Marta home, and she watched Imani eat. They both sat in silence. When most of the plate was gone Imani curled in a bed with a picture of Dave and silently cried.

I miss you, miss you so much. I'm so sorry. Imani missed him and wish she loved him correctly the entire marriage not just some of it. Her heart was heavy, and her eyes were getting heavier.

****

"911 what's your emergency?"

"Yes, my name is Rosalyn, and I just found my daughter in law in bed dead."

"Is she breathing?"

"No!" Mama Ross exclaimed

"When is the last time you or anyone seen her alive?"

"Two days ago at my son's funeral. Please hurry and send someone. She's an aids victim!"

"Mam keep calm. I'm trying my best to assist you. What's the address?" The dispatcher asked.

Could it have been her illness that killed her or was it grief? Just maybe she really did love my son? Maybe she died of a broken heart?

The end!

Epilogue

Talking to the EMT's Mama Ross seemed so grief-stricken. All this death isn't natural. She watched the EMT's gather up the last of their equipment and roll away Imani's lifeless body to be sent to the coroner. A grin sneakily crept across Mama Ross face knowing that bitch is in hell.

I told Imani before fuck with my business or my sons heart I will personally end ya life. My name is Mama Ross, and I keep my promises.

Questions for the reader

1. When was the perfect time for Imani to have told Dave the truth?

2. Did Mama Ross and Caesar help or hinder Dave by keeping him sheltered?

3. What three lessons could you pin point in this book?

4. What subject matters are in this book?

5. Could you have forgiven Imani?

6. Were Dave and Imani really in love or in lust?

7. Was Mama Ross wrong for including Imani in the family business?

8. Who do you think damaged Imani the most?

9. Did Ryan love Imani?

10. How often do you believe that Imani protected herself?

64669092R00139

Made in the USA
Charleston, SC
05 December 2016